3To: Arthur.

Happy Chin

Best wishes.

Jim Crocker

Oct. 2022

UNBIDDEN

By John Winkler

First Impressions

ISBN 9798750093311

Publisher: Sharp Pencils Press, Cheshire UK

Artwork and design by Anna and Jez de Silva

Author's note

The significant events described in the book and the main characters are real. The majority of the stories told are gathered via family record or information passed on to the next generation. The rest is fiction, hopefully reflecting the spirit and nature of the individuals concerned.

UNBIDDEN

PROLOGUE

I was brought up in a simple mining village and lived on a street with no name. Looking back that might seem a bit strange but I gave no thought to it at the time. We were just a number but so was everyone else.

There were just three long rows of terraced houses, two up, two down, with an outside toilet in the yard and a brick coal shed. Although cramped in the house, at the back we had a big garden where my parents grew vegetables and raised chickens.

Whilst my Dad was alive and earning miner's wages, we had more than enough money to lead a good life. Our school was just a short walk up the hill, towards the woods. The woods were a brilliant place to play for children, with ancient trees and lots of hiding places. The pit and its winding gear dominated the entrance to the village but all around was greenery and fields with lots of space and the freedom to play safely in the fresh air.

Our road backed onto the bus station that received the scores of miners at various times of day. This then led directly onto the pit. When the buses had gone the bus station became our sports field, where we would play games such as "kick out can" or "nipsey". We would invent our own games which were generally quite dangerous, or maybe that was just how we liked to play. We were lucky in those days as kids. Our parents could let us out of the house at any time knowing that we would be safe.

I always felt a bit different from the other children, mainly because my dad was German and I was being brought up in the immediate post war years. I suppose I was too young in my infancy to pick up the animosity that I suspect my father must have experienced immediately after his release from the labour camp.

By the time I was old enough to sense any of this I suppose my Dad had become accepted both at work in the pit and in the village. Nevertheless, I was different and I had a German surname. As I grew up, and following trips as a child to Germany, I began to learn about the many privations experienced by the German side of my family. The conventional teaching on the history of the war has tended to be told in black and white terms. You were on one side or another, and generally one side was good and the other bad. For the participants and their families on both sides the reality was much different. Across Europe, before, during and after the war, many thousands of people unwittingly found themselves dragged into a conflict not of their own making and unfairly punished for sins they did not commit.

My visits to see my German family and the many discussions I had with my aunts, uncles and cousins over there made me realise just how difficult but nonetheless amazing our family's lives had been during the Second World War years and its aftermath.

For me the starkest time was the day I was taken down the road to number 62, just five doors away. I had been in that house many times before because one of my best friends lived there. What I couldn't work out was why I was visiting in the middle of the day and why we were allowed to play Subbuteo during school hours.

I was a pretty grown up seven-year-old at the time, as indeed most of us were coming from this background. However, it was difficult to take in let alone understand the consequences of the message my heartbroken Mum tried to convey to me later that day.

So, let the members of the family reveal their experiences. Theirs is a story full of pathos, of horror and salvation.

Main Characters

Johann, Sophie, Sara and Marie Winkler

Hans Flagner

Part 1

Johann

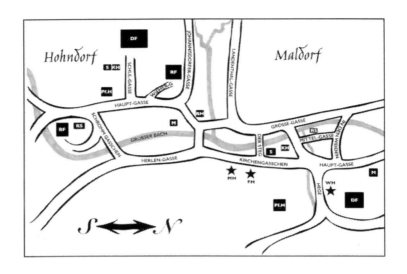

Legend: 1945

RH - Town Hall

S   - German School

RS   - Romanian School

KH - Culture House

Pf.H - Vicarage

M   - Mill

DF - German Cemetery

RF - Romanian Cemetery

WH - Winkler House

FH - Flagner House

MH - Maria's House

(1988)

Chapter One

Maldorf, Rumania 1935

I so loved my childhood home. I used to sit on the single bench by the school in the square in Maldorf, thinking about the village's long history. I was so taken by the fact that there had been a Saxon community here since the thirteenth century and like all of my contemporaries, felt proud of this heritage. The village was right in the heart of the region which we called Siebenbergen, but which was known to the outside world as Transylvania. Externally the area had come to fame through the novels of Bram Stoker who had based his famous character of Dracula on a former character from this area. It had also been characterised in early silent movie versions of the story, but of course there were no vampires in our life as we grew up. At school we had been taught about this but in a very dismissive way and it had been made clear that we were to ignore such trivia.

There were approximately eight hundred people living in Maldorf at this time, mostly dependant on farming and rural pursuits for a living. It used to be a very prolific wine-growing area and you could still see evidence of this from the overgrown terraces on the side of the surrounding hills. The village sat in the foothills of the Carpathians and the nearest thing we had to the Dracula story was the existence of real wolves still living in the mountains. We could occasionally hear them howling in the distance at night but they kept their distance. The distant mountains remain a wild environment and there is talk of brown bears still existing there in the most remote parts.

This sounds very exciting, but in reality Maldorf was a pretty ordinary place with fairly normal amenities. Our village sat alongside the neighbouring community of Hohndorf, separated by a small tributary of the Grosser Bach river. On a map we were so close together you would have thought that we were just one place, and although we shared some facilities, the residents of each village were fiercely loyal to their own community. There were two schools, one for the Saxons and one for the Rumanian children. We shared a church and a Kulturhaus, a sort of village hall which doubled up as an occasional meeting place and dance-hall. There was a priest's house next to the church and also a small Rathaus where our elected leaders met on a regular basis. The two villages clung to their individuality but our communities co-existed quite peaceably most of the time. Perhaps the only exception to this might have been the occasional Saturday night dances when the usual macho tendencies could spill over into fights amongst the boys. These were usually to do with bragging rights and showing off in front of the girls.

The small number of streets dotted around the river were populated by quaint red-tiled houses. There were separate graveyards for native Rumanian families and the Saxon community. Generations of our brethren had been buried there over the centuries. Some of the larger properties like ours had gates leading on to a big courtyard with a large garden at the back where the family were able to farm and grow all that they needed to live. We had a few animals including pigs and chickens. It was fundamentally a small-holding. Some in the village were artisans and had skills that could be sold further afield; carpenters, locksmiths and the like. Our father also owned other land and forestry outside the village and employed a couple of young people to work with him. When I was younger, I would occasionally go to see him as I loved the smell of the sawn wood and the sight of trees being felled. While the men were out at work, the day to day tending to the animals and the crops fell to the women.

Other families, without the luxury of a large garden, relied on work outside on a state-owned farm or vineyard. For some this meant setting off in the early hours to get to their place of work, carrying their farming tools over their shoulders.

Looking across the village towards the church where the Easter celebrations are in full flow, I can see my three sisters all dressed in full regional regalia for the parades and festivities which are to follow. They wear their Saxon costumes with pride as did all of their friends. Their costumes are beautifully embroidered, the result of hours of work undertaken by the womenfolk.

Maria was the eldest of my sisters. She was small, quiet-natured and the most reserved of the children. After me,

Sophie was next down. Sensible and reliable, she wore her curly brown hair in bunches and strutted after her sisters like a mother hen. The youngest, Sara, was dark-haired, strikingly pretty, with an impulsive and fiery character. Any trouble that reared its head and she was always the first into action.

Earlier in the day, we had all been in the church to hear the thanksgiving service. The custom was for the women and girls of the village to sit in the pews on the ground floor of the church and the men and boys to sit upstairs in the stalls, peering down on the proceedings. The older men wore Afghan-style coats made of suede leather, with woolly interiors and collars. I never understood this as they were totally unsuitable for the unseasonably mild weather. I had been seated next to my best friend Hans in the church. Throughout our childhood and adolescence, we had been pretty much inseparable and typical boys. I had developed a bit of a reputation amongst the local girls as being the handsome one. This was probably something to do with my dark black hair and swarthy skin. I was tall and slim, with blue eyes and strikingly long eyelashes. The girls just loved my eyelashes, but if I'm honest I shied away from their attentions.

By contrast, Hans was strong, stocky and thick set, quiet and thoughtful. He was just the sort of friend you needed in your gang when the going got tough! These must have been some of the qualities that my sister Sophie had admired in him but I also think that she was drawn by his calm nature and kind disposition. She wouldn't have admitted it in her earlier years, but I knew that she had long felt a passion for Hans. Our families were very close and we had grown up knowing each other and playing together as children. I didn't let on to Hans, because it might have appeared that I was soft, but I was very pleased that he and my sister gradually grew close to each other. I just liked to watch on and let the romance blossom. Not that I didn't fancy the girls as there were one or two real stunners in the village, but I preferred to be admired by them as a group. No, I wasn't vain, I just knew that they liked how I looked and there was always someone trying to hook me.

As well as the usual religious festival at Easter we had a local tradition whereby the boys who fancied someone would leave a light in the window to attract a girl of their choice. I suppose it let them know of their feelings and the girl would then wear a flower in their hair. I don't know where this had originated, but it obviously went back a long time as our parents used to encourage it and talk of when they went through the process. I didn't bother with it, but on this occasion, Hans had put a lamp in the window and I knew that Sophie had responded as the next day she was resplendent in her costume with a beautiful primrose in her hair.

A short while before in the church, Hans and I had been typically mischievous. From the balcony we had been throwing paper aeroplanes at my three sisters sitting below with the older women. Our actions did not go unnoticed by our parents and we knew that we would be in trouble later, but clearly had felt it was worth it at the time. After the festival the girls had gone back home to change, having then arranged to meet another friend, Katherina, later in the fields at the back of the village. Katherina was the younger sister of Hans, slender and frail. The other girls had a protective relationship with her, as she was very shy and had a tendency to get picked on at school.

Later we went home to help our parents with the various tasks of the day. Not even a major festival could stop the daily needs of the family farm. We boys would help our fathers with the more physical tasks associated with the animals and the crops. If we were lucky, we might be allowed to watch the men brew their home-made schnapps when they came together each month, sharing their different bits of equipment that made up the still. We weren't allowed to taste the produce of course, but it was fascinating to see how their fire-water was made. The girls helped their mothers with cooking, sewing, making wine and looking after the smaller animals. Once the daily tasks were done, by and large our lives were easy-going and fun. Alongside the day to day work we had inherited a strong culture of learning and after our evening meal we would read and do our homework fastidiously. None of us were particularly musical although there was a strong tradition within the wider family. Our uncle George was a fine organist in the church and had a grand piano in his house. Some evenings we would be invited around to hear him play and eat and drink together.

When we were out playing, so long as we steered clear of the wine terraces, we could play in the fields and forests that surrounded the village. Usually, the girls met up in the fields first and then went off to the woods. Sometimes they would gather daisies on the way and lie down by the side of the river to plait them into chains. Sara told me that they talked about the boys and how boorish we were. I think that they pretended to hate us boys but, in reality, they were generally curious to know where we were and what we were up to. Secretly, Sophie had a crush on Hans, whereas Sara fancied all of the boys!

That day we were about a hundred yards up from them along the river bank. We had been play-fighting with sticks and pretend guns, but now the girls could hear us laughing and shouting as we swung across the river on our makeshift swings. We had found a disused tractor tyre in a local farmyard and tied a thick rope to it and secured it to a strong overhanging tree branch at one side of the stream. The girls had crept up on us, watching from a distance. They wouldn't admit it but I suspect they were secretly admiring our daring as we leapt onto the tyre and swung from bank to bank.

Suddenly, the girls burst into fits of laughter as Hans misjudged a jump and went headlong into the river. He turned, embarrassed and completely soaked, and then angrily shouted to me to get the girls. Their laughter just increased as Hans hopelessly tried to extricate himself from the water, assisted by myself and diverting me from the chase. By the time the two of us were on the bank again the girls had long gone. Undaunted, we reverted to our play-fighting, using fallen branches as swords as we pretended to fight for king and country. Hans was dripping wet, but he didn't give a damn. How ironic it would be that a few years later we would be dragged into a real war not of our own making.

The sisters and Katharina had their own mischievous games. Some days they would play hide and seek amongst the trees and bushes and tease the single lonely herdsman who tended the herd of water buffalo on behalf of the village. He was called Wolfgang and in his late teens. His was a very important job for the village and so he didn't take kindly to the girl's distractions. Each family would have at least one male and one female buffalo and early in the morning the beasts would be released onto the street and then wander unaided to the centre of the village where they would join the rest of the herd. Wolfgang would gently gather them and the animals would then follow him, ambling slowly into the foothills where they grazed for the rest of the day. Later in the afternoon he would encourage them to retrace their steps back towards the village and then they would find their own way back to their homes, as if by some form of sixth sense.

Just thinking about this reminds me of a very funny incident that occurred a bit later on in my life. We were being visited by one of the Volksgruppe members. The Volksgruppe had been imposed on the village in the mid-thirties and taken over the duties that were once done so effortlessly by our local elected leaders. As the National Socialists in Germany began to exert wider controls, they had appointed their supporters locally to administer on their behalf. They were very officious and would often just call in unannounced to reinforce some ruling that had been passed down from above. What happened that day became a constant source of amusement for the family and would be relived time and time again.

Our house had a big double-fronted gate which opened out onto a large courtyard. We opened and shut the gate at appropriate times for the returning animals. At that time our female buffalo had recently given birth to a calf which was housed in the barn at the rear of the courtyard. It was late afternoon and the officious visitor had been oblivious to the local habits of the animals. Neither had my parents thought to warn them about the return of the buffaloes. The man had just arrived late in the afternoon and as it was boiling hot, he was drawing water from the well in the courtyard. Suddenly, without warning, the brooding female buffalo came hurtling into the yard through the open gates, desperate to get back to her calf. At the last minute the man saw the danger and threw himself out of the way and fell to the ground in a heap. As he angrily dusted himself down, the male buffalo ambled into the yard and slowly took a drink from the water trough at his side, ignoring the bemused visitor. Disdainfully the buffalo then walked slowly to join his family down the yard. The unfortunate visitor just stood there looking totally confused and shaken by the incident.

Chapter Two

1940 – National Service

As the decade had worn on my friendship with Hans had continued to strengthen and we were pretty much inseparable. He had in the meantime become very close with my sister Sophie and the two spent any spare time together walking in the countryside and doing the normal things that young sweethearts do. In May, during the Fasching festival in the village, Sophie had made sure that none of the other girls got hold of Hans. During this time, it was the tradition that the girls could pick who they wanted from the boys. A strange bit of role reversal I suppose, but the festival was generally a chance for the whole community to let their hair down. For these few days there was dancing and drinking and lively gatherings in the square, with the local band playing traditional tunes.

I was so pleased that they were together and to see my sister looking even happier than normal. While Hans was with Sophie, it left me with more time to hang out with the other young men in the village and we would meet up in the evenings to chat and have a drink together. By now I was old enough to share the home-grown schnapps and get involved in the banter.

Most of the others also smoked their cigarettes, but I never took to this disgusting habit. It would have been fashionable for me to smoke just to join in, but I wasn't one for doing something just for the sake of it. I remember when I was about seven years old my grandad had given me a drag of his cigarette and it had made me cough and feel sick. From that moment on I had never wanted to join in when the lads at school went illicitly at break time to catch a crafty smoke. This had obviously been a cunning ploy from my grandad to put me off smoking and it had worked. Strangely enough he had tried the same tactics by offering me a drink of his beer at the same age, but it had probably had the opposite effect as now I was at the head of the queue when we met and cracked open a few bottles of beer to go with the schnapps.

I continued to help my family out with the farming side of our life and occasionally got the chance to help my Dad in the forest to supplement our income. Hans in the meantime got himself a job with the Romanian police with the help of our cousin Rosina. Although her political influence had gone, she still had good contacts in some places. A short time later, Hans and I were called up to do a six-month stint of national service. We had seen others go off in earlier years and weren't worried about this because it was seen as a bit of a doddle according to those who had done it before. It meant time away from the family which was the only drawback, particularly for Hans and Sophie. I hadn't a steady girl-friend and although I had done my bit of kissing and canoodling with the girls in the village, I rather enjoyed the army life and the exercise that went with it. We were sent to a camp near to Timisoara and on our time off we were able to visit this beautiful city. I had never before really had time to appreciate life outside our village and it was good to see the ornate buildings and meet people from different backgrounds.

Initially we took some ribbing about our Saxon heritage from the mainly Rumanian contingent, some of whom were quite frankly roughnecks. Having Hans as a friend helped me when the ribbing threatened to get out of hand, because it didn't take them long to work out that he was tougher than them. We both took to the mock-military regime. Training, marching, parading and getting to try out the weaponry was all new to us and seemed a bit of a game really. However, nearing the end of the training, just before we were due to return home, we picked up information within the camp about the war being fought further afield in France and Belgium. The hardened soldiers who had been our trainers pulled our legs and joked that we wouldn't be going home and that we would instead be sent to fight against the Allies. Our government had changed position so many times we weren't even sure whose side we were supposed to be on so the jibes went nowhere with Hans, who was always ready to give back.

-   Get lost you idiot. I'm ready for anything mate, don't worry about that, but I can't see us getting involved. The President of the Council of Ministers has got splinters in his arse from sitting on the fence so much.

Although he had put it crudely it was true. We had no idea

at that time how things were developing further afield. There had been no attempt to politicise any of us throughout the training and no discussion about the Romanian army's part in the wider conflict. We were like tin toy soldiers playing at war. Little did we know what was to unfold.

Only a few of our young people chose to join up for the war in Europe after national service. Most of us when we got back to our villages just got on with life as if nothing had changed. We were straight back into our work on the farm and into our old routines. As the weeks and months passed Hans and Sophie resumed their romance and began to think ahead. Eventually Hans asked her to marry, Dad agreed and plans were laid for them to tie the knot late in 1943.

Meanwhile Sara seemed also to be settling down. She was no longer getting herself involved with different boys in the village and had developed a relationship with a lad called Martin. I had a very open relationship with Sara and knew I could speak plainly with her. She generally went about life in a care-free manner, and was quite naturally uninhibited in the way she dealt with the world. I knew Martin mainly by reputation and he became part of an older set and had become a bit of a tearaway. This is probably what attracted him to Sara because she was always interested in things that were a bit different or more exciting. I tried to tell her plainly about getting too close to him and she was forthright in letting me know that she would follow her heart. At least I had tried, and I took no pleasure in watching things develop. As I had feared, it didn't work out that great for her, because she became pregnant and hasty plans had to be put into place for them to get married. It caused a bit of a stir in both sets of family at the time and I could see that although eventually our parents rallied round to support her, she was getting a lot of grief from Martin's mother.

Johann, Hans and Martin, 1942

Chapter Three

Maldorf - August 1943

One fateful morning I woke up to find an official looking letter laying on the kitchen table. I looked at my parents anxiously as they waited for me to open it. I read it and was stopped dead in my tracks. At first, I didn't know what to say, then I blurted out:

- I've only been conscripted into the German army. Good God, I thought I'd done my bit of service in the Rumanian army and that would be it. This can't be right.

My mind flashed back a couple of years when we had been given the opportunity to volunteer to join the German army in the war against the Allies, but only a handful of young people from some of the neighbouring villages had chosen to go down this route. Now it would seem we were to be given no choice.

By and large there had been a great deal of scepticism about the war in Europe within the community. Our elected local leaders at the time, including my aunt Rosina, had kept a distance from the conflict and we respected their views. Lately, however, they had had to be very careful as the Volksgruppe were by now were all-powerful having been appointed by the German state. Looking back, perhaps if earlier we had taken more time to look at what had been going on in the outside world, the unfolding events would not have come as such a shock. Perhaps at the time we didn't ask enough questions about what was going on in the war. Maybe our local councillors were too protective? It's quite strange now looking back and asking myself all these questions. How had we got ourselves into this position? Were we somehow complicit in the horrors of war and in the atrocities carried out by our German leaders? I do know that at the time of my call up the last thing I wanted to do was to go to war. Up to this time I hadn't developed any real interest in what had been happening in Europe. It was only later, when the dust had settled, that I could identify what really happened and why. I keep thinking that maybe that is how history is for the masses and why somehow the ruthless ambitions of leaders go unchallenged?

For my own part I was a little bemused at why we were at war with Britain in the first place. What little we knew about the British was that they had become allies again with other European states just as had happened in the horror years of the Great War. There was nothing worthwhile to listen to on the Rumanian radio broadcasts and so we had listened in on the BBC Empire Service. This was our only way of having some knowledge of the world outside of Rumania. From this we had come to understand that Hitler's ambitions lay in Poland and the east, so for us to be called up to fight the British seemed ridiculous. We had come to see the British as civilised friends, not enemies to go to war with. It didn't help that our hapless governments kept switching allegiance as events infolded.

Having reacted to the contents of the letter, I pleaded with my parents to stop this happening. In the past, from when I could remember, if we had any trouble our parents could sort it out. This was very different, as my Dad made me instantly realise.

- Sorry son, there's nothing I can do. You can't say no to this. This is a very clear instruction and comes right from the top. We can have a word with Rosina but the local community council has no say now. I guess you'll just have to do what you're being told.

I stormed out of the house and went straight around to see Hans. He was as shocked as me and had received the same news and response from his father. We retreated to the village square for a drink with the locals and perhaps to hear a little sympathy from them. We had often gone there and sat back and had a laugh as we listened in to the banter of the older generation in particular. They used to go on about the last war, so I guess we expected a bit of sympathy.

- What's up misery-guts. What's with the sour face?

One of them asked us. We explained about the call up letters.

We had picked up from their earlier discussions that there were mixed feelings in the village about the war being fought in Europe. In the past we had heard Gunther, who was one of the older villagers we mixed with, saying how he had fought in the Great War and how he retained bitter memories from his earlier experiences. Now in his early fifties, he was in the camp of those who still felt angry about how Germany had been treated after the Great War.

- Come on lads you've got the chance to help Hitler get Germany back to where it was as a proud nation. I read that he had said that the Jews have been milking the country dry. You youngsters should be proud to support him so that he can win the war. I think he is struggling to hold the buggers off now and needs our help.'

I wasn't amused by this.

- It's easy for you to say. It's not you who has to go off and leave your family behind. I don't give a toss about the war and what about Hans, he's supposed to be getting married soon?

Another of the older group decided to jump in. Willie was a bit more in the know and like my Aunt Rosina had been a former community leader. More recently he had been trying to influence the Voksgruppe without much effect.

- Look, we knew things were heating up by the way they have been talking to us. We have been trying to keep the village out of any conflict and didn't want to upset people unnecessarily. I suppose we were hoping it would go away. Maybe we should have been talking more about this instead of pretending we could keep our village out of the war. Anyway, I'm sorry it has come to this but it's too late now to say no to these people as they clearly are acting on orders from the Fuehrer.

Hans chipped in angrily.

- So, you mean you have known about this for some time and haven't told us? You could at least have given us some warning. I would have made my plans to marry Sophie earlier, but now we aren't going to be able to go ahead. In any case what has all this got to do with us in Rumania?

Willie did his best to explain, but it fell on deaf ears.

- We think that Hitler is getting more and more desperate for troops as he is fighting on too many fronts. He won't admit it but he is losing the war. We probably have been seduced by propaganda and talk about how we were winning the war. As I said, we hoped it would be over soon and we could stay out of it but now things have changed and we can't avoid getting involved. You'll have to hope it's all over before you get to the front. There is maybe a slim chance that he will sign up for peace, but I wouldn't hold your breath.

Hans blew up at this.

- What about our wedding? How can I leave Sophie behind? She is so set on getting married. I'm not fucking going. They will have to fight me first.

Gunther responded angrily:

- For Christ's sake stop your moaning. Just what sort of talk is that? You should feel proud that you are being given the chance to fight for your country. I'd jump at the chance if I wasn't past it now.

Willie sensed that Hans was about to explode and urged:

- Whatever you feel Hans, you can't fight this. Hitler is struggling and he's calling up Germans in communities from all over Europe. It's not just Maldorf, there are thousands of what he has called the Volksdeutsch in many different countries. No-one can escape this, but I'm hoping it will all be over soon. Let's just pray that they'll see sense.

Hans stormed off and I chased after him to offer some consolation. Although I was angry, I took some comfort from Willie's words. Maybe the war would end soon anyway. How wrong could I be? Just two weeks later we were being shoved unceremoniously into trucks, and driven off with the few items of clothing that we had put together. My parents were there to see me off and poor Sophie waved us goodbye with tears streaming down her face.

Initially we were mustered in Hermanstadt with loads of

other young people from neighbouring towns and villages. From there we endured a long train journey heading towards South Germany where we were to undergo our brief military training in Munich. Because of the distance involved we stayed overnight in Hungary, in tents which we had to erect on route. I couldn't get to sleep initially, and recall how strange it felt to have left the village and suddenly seeming to be so close to war.

When we finally arrived at the training-camp we clung onto our belongings, frightened and not knowing what the future might hold. We were issued with uniforms, gas mask, gas cape, a Karabiner 98 rifle and a sidearm. Suddenly the war had become real. Within months, we would be serving on the front and experiencing the horrors of the war. Unable to sleep, the same questions kept coming back to haunt me. Whose war was this anyway and why were we fighting the British? I felt terrible for Hans too as I knew that he was missing Sophie badly. Every time I looked at him, he cut a sad figure and it was difficult to get him to engage in any conversation. One bit of good news was that having made a plea to his chief officer he was granted compassionate leave and allowed briefly to return to Maldorf to marry Sophie. Then it was off into the unknown.

Chapter Four

Aachen - October 1944

Somehow, I had managed to survive the war so far. Hans and I had been separated after the initial training camp and I had no way of knowing whether he was still alive or not. I was completely exhausted like all of my pals as we had been dragged across France and Belgium chasing shadows. Now for some reason we were near to Aachen. As usual our officers had told us the absolute minimum about why we were there and we had marched for days before we set up camp. It wouldn't have been so bad if we had been properly fed, but our rations had become increasingly inedible. We were all cold and wet and thoroughly miserable! I couldn't get out of my head the earlier sight of one of our company with his head smashed to smithereens during a mortar attack. Until you have experienced death like this the war just seems like a bad dream. Now it is a bloody nightmare and everyone is waiting for their turn to die.

I remember huddling closely with my new friend Jakub in the corner of the pillbox. He was another "Volksdeutsch", but from Poland. He had also been suddenly conscripted from his small village, and given our similar experiences we had developed a close relationship. We had to be careful in our conversations as our cynicism about the war was not shared by the vast majority in the troop who were mainland Germans and generally supporters of the cause.

- I don't like where this is going Johann. It doesn't feel right. We haven't a cat in hells chance of rescuing that lot from over the bridge.
- I know, and I'm worried about the secret huddles our so-called leaders keep having amongst themselves. Have you noticed how they have stopped telling us what is going on?

Looking back on what had been happening in the weeks and days before we arrived at Aachen, the campaign had been a bitter and bloody one as our troop seemed to move around the battlefront in a completely meaningless way. In the early days we had been bombarded with lots of positive propaganda about how we were winning the war and how Europe would soon be in German control, but none of that impressed us now.

I had never had any real affinity with the cause, and typically the Volksdeutsch from the outside "colonies", as it were, had a different take on this from those who had been living in Germany at the time war broke out. These home-landers generally retained much enthusiasm and we Volksdeutschers quickly learned to show our own sympathy to the cause, otherwise we knew there would be repercussions. We had witnessed individuals being punished severely for expressing doubts about the campaign.

- Jakub, I'm getting so pissed off thinking about all the colleagues we have lost. The only way I can cope at the moment is to think of my family and friends back in Maldorf and try to remember the happy times we had as kids.

-   I'm the same. I just keep thinking about my wife and our little boy back home. God, I hope I make it through the war so that I can see him again.

As the war had proceeded, as well as losing many of our colleagues from the constant barrage that took place wherever we were fighting, we had also seen a number who had succumbed to the sheer hard work and fatigue of the marching and digging hide-outs. So, there we were, dug in again, feeling like cannon fodder, fighting someone else's war. We'd been stuck there for days. Over the early years of the war any minute sense of loyalty to the cause had been sucked out of us. The shelling had been interminable and day by day our losses had increased. In the mornings we were continually attacked by fighter bombers and we also came under attack most days from heavy artillery, grenade launchers and automatic weapons. The noise was deafening and the fighter planes came over so low that they almost seemed to touch us. The worst thing was the psychological effect of the trench mortars as we couldn't see them and we didn't hear them until they exploded around us.

I sensed it was getting towards the end of the war, but nobody was sure at all what was happening with the bigger picture. We just got a load of crap from our officers. Up until our arrival in Aachen we seemed to have been walking for hours in the days immediately past. We had been told eventually that our task was to relieve a battalion of comrades who were under siege near Aachen. When we got to the outskirts of the town it was clear that we were fighting a lost cause. What seemed like a whole army of Allied troops could be seen in the distance, but our senior officers seemed oblivious to the situation that we were facing. We had never experienced the kind of good leadership that transcends the horrors of war and creates a sense of togetherness through adversity. We didn't know exactly, but we imagined the British had this in spades.

Our senior officers had long found it difficult to hide their sense of inadequacy and we had stopped advancing long ago. We just seemed to be going around in circles, and being pressed back into an ever-decreasing and inhospitable tract of land. Our move towards Aachen seemed like a last desperate move. It didn't help our cause when earlier in the course of the fighting we had been bombarded by Allied propaganda leaflets. These had been constantly dropped on us by the Allies, with messages translated into German. Initially we just ignored them, but as our plight got worse, they began to succeed in undermining us. In the end they confirmed in our minds what we already knew, that we were losing the war.

The last batch came at the wrong time for us really, towards the end. They had subtle messages that just hit home and confirmed what many of us were feeling about fighting a lost cause that we had never bought into.

I recall clearly even now three of these leaflets and the messages they contained. One was headed "Sturheit", which I think is "obstinacy" in English. I guess this was a clever way of undermining what was commonly seen by outsiders as a particular quality of the German soldier. The leaflet argued that to show such a quality when the war was clearly being lost was futile. It said that the country at home was in flames through sustained bombing campaigns on our cities and that carrying on amounted to criminal indifference, apathy and short-sightedness.

Another leaflet I remember, said that by continuing to fight we were deliberately prolonging the war and adding to the plight of people at home. This "Kieggvelangerer" leaflet argued that despite our undoubted bravery we could do something more useful as individuals to stop this slaughter by surrendering. The final one, headed "Bericht Aus Westdeutschland", translated literally as a report from Germany, emphasised the negative effect that continuing the war would have on the reconstruction of Germany after the war.

I have no doubt in my mind that these slowly dripping comments had the desired effect and finally, when our commanding officers fled in the night, we quickly got together and decided enough was enough. We fashioned our white flags from the stained sheets we huddled under at night time, threw our weapons over the top and raised our arms in surrender. We were fortunate that when we raised the flags our enemy took pity on us and resisted the temptation to mow us down as we slowly emerged from our foxholes. I remember feeling shit-scared as we edged forward towards the American troops with their guns pointing directly at us. We hadn't eaten properly for days and must have looked a real rabble as they took control of us. We were pretty relieved because we had heard stories of American troops taking retribution on prisoners, but thankfully we were soon handed over to British forces who then took responsibility for us.

Once we were handed over to the British, we were given clear orders what to do, but their decency and muted compassion was hardly deserved. Nevertheless, we were grateful for the modicum of kindness shown as we were taken away.

- Keep your hands up Fritz. Move over there and keep quiet!

We were more than happy to oblige and did exactly as we were told. Their apparent decency, however, didn't stop them from taking our watches and anything of value as prizes of war. Our swastika badges on our uniforms seemed to be of particular interest to them, presumably as spoils of the war to show their kids in the future.

Our officers had fed us with hatred and scared us with stories about the awful things that would happen if we were caught, so this actual experience was a relief. Although I was a bit wary about the next stages, in reality the early journey in the guarded vehicles wasn't so bad. It felt a bit muted as the English guards kept a firm watch over us, and sure, they hurled a few profanities at us, but once they realised that we were passive and relieved prisoners, they relaxed and gave us the odd cigarette. We had been forced to climb in great numbers into the back of trucks and the driver then took off at breakneck speed, presumably to stop any thoughts of escape. This couldn't have been further from my mind as I was just relieved to be out of the conflict.

Away from the battlefield we were stripped of any documentation and personal items such as photographs. Our pay books and letters also provided them with information which presumably helped them later when we were under interrogation. The information told them where our unit fitted into the wider campaign and also gave them the basis for beginning to determine the strength of our allegiance to the Nazi cause. Initially we were gathered together in fields which served as temporary holding areas. There was no shelter available and no food and drink for a while. Eventually we were given a basic ration pack with powdered tea and milk, artificial sweetener, plus the boiling water to generate a much-needed drink.

We were then taken first to a camp in Mecklenburg and had to undergo a preliminary interrogation. At this stage they just wanted to check paperwork and ask basic questions about where we came from and what we thought about the war. From here after a couple of days we were taken by truck to another holding camp at Erdingen, which

I think was near Brussels.

After this we were again moved on very quickly to the port of Ostend to be transported to England for eventual re-settlement into more permanent camps. I found out at a later date that this fitted in with the Geneva Conference requirements for prisoners to be removed as soon as possible from the battlefield to a place of safety. Looking back at this it explained the degree of civility that we were shown throughout the process of capture, for which we were all extremely grateful.

We were transported across the Channel on boats which they referred to as LST vessels. Again, I later found out that these were formally named Landing Ships, Tank. I assume that they were the type of ship which helped to land their troops on the continent to fight the war on mainland Europe. I recall that the port we landed at was Tilbury. On disembarkation we were marched a short distance to a railway platform and onto reasonably comfortable carriages with seats and different compartments. This quite surprised us all as during the conflict, if we weren't marching, when we were being transported further afield by our own commanders, we were taken in effectively what were cattle trucks!

On arrival in England, we spent a few days being questioned in a holding camp, which I think was at a place called Kempton Park in the south of England. It was a very elegant park of sorts with splendid grandstands and pavilions. There was an extensive race track bordered by neat white fences which made me think that it was mainly used as a racecourse for horses in peacetime. During the time I was there I noticed that about four trains a day would arrive, each carrying a few hundred prisoners of war. Looking back, although it was a relatively short length of time that we were at Kempton Park, there was a lot going on in the process. Initially on arrival we were searched again, fed, medically examined, bathed and then re-clothed in our disinfected original clothing. This was very wise as over time most of us soldiers had become infested with lice. I can't describe how good it felt after taking a shower, even though the water was stone cold!

I remember being taken for interrogation. I assume that the prime purpose of this was to decide where I would be sent for more permanent accommodation. The prospect of interrogation in itself was a frightening one as I knew the sort of processes that the Gestapo used. Thankfully what I got was less harrowing, but nonetheless very thorough and clever. From the various pieces of documentation, photographs and letters they had taken from each of us they were able to skilfully ascertain our attitudes and what level of threat we might pose. I eventually ended up in low security camp, attached to a farm, so they must have been reassured that I was not a threat to them. It is true that I wasn't in any way politicised or driven by the Nazi cause and thankfully this came through in my interviews. At the end of the process, I was told that I was to be transported to the north of England, to a place in Yorkshire.

As Hans and I had been allocated to different divisions at the start of our service I had no idea what had happened to him. Whilst we were in training for the war, we had discussed this and Hans and I had agreed that if we survived the war, we would try to meet up back in South Germany where we had undertaken our military training. We had done our initial training near to Munich and had been impressed by what we had seen of the area. My last time with Hans before we were sent off to war, was when we were issued by the Red Cross with a kitbag. This consisted of a shirt, a pair of underpants, two pairs of socks, one toothbrush, one comb, a bar of soap and a sewing kit. Also included were six cigarettes, a small quantity of tobacco, and our own personal set of knife, fork and spoon

Now stuck in England waiting to be taken to a camp, my anxiety levels were pretty high. Weeks of capture, interrogation and moving around were suddenly starting to take their toll. Just what did the future hold for me, and would I ever see my family again?

Picture of the ex-POW huts at Woolley, taken 2019

Chapter Five

Haigh, South Yorkshire - February 1945

After a journey by coach of about six hours, the group of prisoners that I had been placed with arrived at a makeshift camp at the top of a steep hill in a village called Haigh in South Yorkshire. I was one of forty or so prisoners of war who tumbled out of the coaches, and who were then led by guards to the two huts that had been recently converted to house us. The camp was off the beaten track and down a narrow un-made road. I guess the plan had been to make this as remote and as low key as possible so as not to stir up any anti-German sentiments from the locals. We found out that the wider area was known locally as Woolley Edge, a surprisingly green and pleasant escarpment, which was apparently a place where courting couples would meet in happier times.

I remember looking out of the bus window as we approached the camp and being struck at just how the landscape looked so similar to my homeland. The rolling hills, the woodland and the open fields. True, the strange high wheel and dark black mounds in the valley were a bit of a giveaway that there was some kind of industry at the heart of this community. It was only later that I found out that we were just a few miles from the town of Barnsley which was at the centre of the South Yorkshire mining industry. Despite the stark surroundings of the mine and in particular the monumental winding gear at the centre of the village, my eyes were drawn wider afield beyond the industrial waste where the countryside oozed a certain splendour and beauty.

-   Ok, we are here now you scruffy lot. Jump out and form a line.

We had picked up enough of the language in the previous weeks since our capture to know what to do when the guard barked out his instructions at us. We were shepherded towards the two huts that seemed to have been made out of corrugated metal. Randomly, we were split into two groups of twenty and allocated a specific hut. Moving into the first hut, I noted the rather spartan features. Inside there were a number of two-tier bunks with straw mattresses supported by a wire grid. The only other furniture in the room were two large tables and four benches. Once in the room we were each issued with two grey blankets and shown how to make up the bed.

In addition to the dormitories also on the site was a toilet block and a separate kitchen and dining area. We found out in time that the small camp had been transformed from what was formerly a base for a local Scout group into a labour camp for non-political prisoners of war. It dawned on me just how few guards there had been on arrival and I guessed that we were all considered to be a low threat and therefore the camp also had minimal security fencing. We came to learn that the camp commandant was a reasonable man and this meant that the camp was run firmly but fairly.

Until the work on the farm became finalised there was a good deal of leisure time to kill, and for the most part, I found myself sitting on the edge of my bunk wondering what life had in store for me. The guard overseeing our hut had left copies of a magazine called "Wochenpost" for us all to read but initially we tended to be suspicious of it. It had been produced by the British government in the German language and by now we had all got used to taking propaganda with a pinch of salt. Strangely enough I kept a copy of the first edition we were given. It was headed:

Wochenpost, December 1944

Soviet Forces Driving German Army out of Russia

Soviet forces are successfully driving remnants of the German 6th and 8th Armies and their fascist allies towards the Hungarian border.

It went on for several paragraphs more but once I had realised that it was propaganda, I tended not to read on beyond the first sentence or two.

I started to cough from the effects of the all-pervading smell of burning wood and coal from the stove in the centre of the room. I had to squint to read the magazine as the lighting was exceedingly poor throughout the room. The magazine did it's best to present as balanced a point of view on the progress of the war but I remained suspicious. After the first few editions of these magazines, I gave them no more than a cursory glance.

Over time I came to put much greater store about what

was happening in the war through my discussions with the interpreter who was allocated to aid communications between the prisoners and the guards. At least then I could frame the questions. Ironically, the interpreter in this camp was a German Jew who had escaped to England in the early years of Nazism. Surprisingly he seemed to bear no malice to the prisoners and came to be trusted by us over time. He had his own interesting back-story which I was to find out about later when we came to trust each other. One of the first things he did for me was to find out where Hans had been posted so that I could eventually write to him and keep in touch. He was also the one who made the contact back home with Maldorf via the local priest there, Karl Ungar. I was particularly lucky that my home village had this benevolent clergyman who had gone out of his way to provide a conduit for the villagers with their loved ones far from home.

Initially we were allowed to write just one letter a week to our home address. This was limited to a single sheet of paper and we were told to keep to the basics. My main aim was to use this opportunity to reassure my family that I was ok and to give them my address. I told them the little bit that I knew of my location and the habits of the local population, which I gradually got to learn about as time went on. As the weeks passed, I picked up a smattering of English, and gradually, with more exposure to the local population, my language skills improved.

Via my discussions with our interpreter, I learnt about the

big political debate that had taken place in the British parliament about the position of POW's. Initially the discussion had focussed on the potential danger to the population of the large numbers of prisoners held in the country. As the debate unfolded, however, it became recognised that these dangers were minimal and instead that POW's could be an asset which helped meet the country's growing need for food through agriculture. He explained that the German sea blockade had meant that imports of food had been reduced by half and therefore Britain was in danger of running out of supplies. This seemed to have triggered a fear of starvation and had prompted a more enlightened approach to use prisoners in this way. I was doubly lucky in that I had some of the skills needed to assist the local farmers through my experience back home on our small-holding. I think that this quickly became apparent to the farmer who I had been assigned to and was reflected in the way he eventually came to trust me and treat me kindly.

I was the only Volksdeutsch amongst the group working at the farm. The others had been recruited from different parts of Germany. We were a very diverse group in terms of background and interests. Eventually, once we had shown that we could be trusted, we were afforded some privileges. I got to know some friends of the farmer and because I had many practical skills, I came to do odd jobs for them outside the camp.

December 1946

Although officially the process of re-patriating prisoners had begun in September 1946, most were kept on to aid the country's recovery and the process was deliberately slow, I think. Originally, we were paid a pittance of just six shillings for a forty-eight-hour week, which I know was just a fraction of the basic-labourers rate at the time. Slowly over time as our work became more valued our pay increased.

The interpreter kept us up to date with the changing attitudes in the wider world. Initially there had been strict rules imposed about prisoners mixing with the local population, but slowly the rules were relaxed. Our interpreter told me towards the end of 1946 that Secretary of State Bellenger had announced that well-behaved prisoners could take unescorted walks of up to five miles, though trips to pubs and other public places were still banned. Families were informed that they could apply for permission for a prisoner to visit their home and this led to me being invited to join the farmer and his wife for Christmas lunch which I greatly appreciated.

Over time this led to an easing of relationships with the local population but also, I think we were particularly lucky in this area to have a kindly local man called Mr. Rich. He arranged with the Commandant to take us out in our turn to the nearby Miners Institute where we could mix with the villagers, have a beer and a bit of entertainment. By this time also I had started to receive occasional mail from home via the priest in Maldorf. As well as facilitating the exchange of letters, I learnt from my family that he was producing a local news-sheet about the wartime experiences of the various young Maldorf soldiers. Some of course had not survived the war, but there were many like me who were prisoners in different camps and our information was shared with families back home who were anxious for news.

The attitude of the locals towards us prisoners hadn't been all plain sailing. In the early days we had met with some anger from the odd local resident and this carried on for a while. Occasionally some individuals would shout obscenities from the road as we worked in the fields. Over time this subsided and the exposure to the pub by Mr. Rich eventually meant that we were not seen as a threat and that perhaps we were just ordinary people just like them.

Nevertheless. I remember a sense of fore-boding the first time I was taken out by Mr. Rich. I thought that there would be some bad feeling when we entered the Welfare. For the first few visits I felt a bit uncomfortable, but the local miners were a forgiving lot and were happy to see someone like me enjoying their local ale. It was also here that I first saw a local girl about the same age as me called Flo. Her name was in fact Florence but once I got to know her, I realised she liked to be known just as Flo. It took me a couple of visits to the Saturday dance to find this out, but I had immediately spotted her the first time I was there.

She was short and slim with long blond hair and vibrantly laughing blue-green eyes. There were other girls around of course, but I could see that the other boys in the hall gravitated towards her throughout the evening. I didn't dare approach her at this stage but I left feeling happy as I was convinced that she had cast a few furtive glances my way also.

It took me several more weeks to pluck up the courage to speak to her and even longer to ask her to dance. I thought that she would tell me to get lost but no she let me talk with her and initially we exchanged names. I could see that there was some tension in the room from the village boys that were there, but this didn't seem to bother her. Each time I went to the dance we looked out for each other and having taken those first steps things just happened so quickly and we fell head over heels in love. We could only meet very occasionally at this stage but this seemed to cement our relationship more. She told me that at first her parents were against the idea of us being together but a few weeks later she told me that she had persuaded them that they should meet me. I had to apply for permission from the camp officials which was granted. I waited until the weekend when by this time I had most of the day off and I walked the two miles across Woolley edge and then down through the woods to Woolley Colliery village where she lived.

I was lucky I guess that once they had met me, they soon came to see that I was a decent bloke and that I was hardworking and very loyal to their daughter. Her parents were good people and very much typical of the local mining community. Hard working, generous and honest folk who believed strongly in family life. I had been brought up in the same sort of environment and could readily identify with them. From what Flo had said to me not all the villagers felt the same about the relationship and I met a bit of hostility walking back through the village on my way back to the camp. However, it was worth it from my point of view and I worked out that over time it would subside.

It transpired that Flo's father Walt had served in the First World War, and had little of the baggage that some people still had about the current conflict. Once I got to know him, he said he knew how people got unwittingly embroiled in war and how individuals on both sides ended up suffering, win or lose. He was happy go lucky and very generous by nature. I was taken aback the first time we were introduced at the Welfare. He may have had a few reservations still about me but nevertheless he thrust some coins into my hand.

- Hey up lad. Have this will tha. Treat Flo to a Snowball, it's her favourite drink and get thi sen a pint.
- No Walt. Please. I have money.
- Nay, lad, money's made round to go round.

Chapter Six

March 1947 – Woolley Village

After a while, I noticed that because of this generosity and free spirit, Walt had to be constantly brought down to earth by his wife Lucy. She was small in stature, but very forceful. No one got the better of Lucy! Despite what happened during the war, I came to consider myself very lucky at eventually becoming part of their family. I know that this came at a cost initially to them as well as to myself and Florrie. In the early stages of our relationship there were still some people who couldn't reconcile why she would choose a German prisoner of war so soon after the conflict had ended. It was only later, after I had proved myself in the pit with my work colleagues, that they came to realise that I was just like them, an ordinary bloke who had just got caught up in the war.

In the early stages of our relationship, I had got to know more about Flo from our discussions during our long walks in the countryside. She told me that during the war she had spent some time in the ATS. Until she explained this to me, I didn't realise just how much a role that women had played at home while the men were away. She had been sent to work in Manchester, some forty or so miles away and worked in munitions factories and then in the catering corps. When the war had finished, she got some work in bars in the city and told me about the famous professional wrestlers that she got to know there. They must have been attracted to her good looks and she clearly had relished the time there. She told me about their exotic names and that although they might sound as if they came from Eastern Europe or South America, they were from more humble surroundings. I remember her laughing about one who was called the Hungarian Panther.

Giggling, she blurted out;

- Like hell he was. He came from Eccles in Lancashire and had the broadest accent you could hope to hear.

She told me that eventually she got fed up of being away from home and returned to the Barnsley area to work in the local pubs. On one of our meetings, I got to meet her sister Nancy who was the sweetest person you could imagine. While Flo was off picking wild flowers to take home Nancy grabbed hold of me and whispered:

- She's a real catch you know. The local lads are all mad about her. She was like a magnet to the boys when she worked in Manchester. Please look after her, she's worth it.

During these brief visits we would explore the surrounding area, holding hands and sharing the occasional kiss. I was so careful not to overdo things as I was still pinching myself about my luck at being so close to Flo. Regarding her village, the immediate impression that I got was of the industrial heritage of the place. The houses were built of local red brick with grey slate roofs. Two long parallel terraced streets stretched out from the bus station where the miners arrived and then up towards the woods in the distance. The streets had no names and the houses were just identified by their number. At the bottom of the bus station a single rail line ran through to the pit with wagons full of coal ready to be sent by truck to the various outlets. I guessed that would be to dealers and factories and most importantly to the power stations further afield. A bit further on there were stables which housed the pit ponies that were either at the end of their long careers down the mine, or were resting ready for another long stint underground. Some ponies never saw that light of day and spent their whole life underground until they had to be hauled up into the daylight. The local children used to hover around the sidings and the stables and when the buses had gone at night time they would use the bus station as their playground, playing their weird games.

Looking back on my later days in the camp, I might have become more dispirited by some of the bitterness from the locals had it not been for Florrie and her family. As it turned out, I became more thoughtful and philosophical about my experiences and increasingly I came to reflect on the irony of war. I would ask myself who were the winners and who were the losers. I certainly had lost a lot because of the war. I still missed my friends and family back in Rumania, but somehow, I had been given a chance to start a new life. Perhaps I could become a winner again.

As a consequence, when I was released from the camp, I looked forward positively to starting my life again. Most of the prisoners had decided to return home to their families but as I had been lucky to have met a local girl during my stay at the camp I decided to stay in England. The eventual release dates had been put back because we POWs were being seen as increasingly crucial in helping to meet Britain's chronic shortage of food after the war. With so many prisoners still in the community after the war had ended there were still mixed feelings around. Some of the British people had taken positives from our contribution, but there was still a lot of suspicion and hostility in the minds of others.

In the face of this, it might have been easier for me to just take off, but gradually my relationship with Flo had grown, and initially I had to weigh up the options available to me. I had no wife or girlfriend to return to at home and wasn't sure whether re-patriation would be to communist controlled Rumania or Germany. Thankfully, as I became surer about my feelings for Flo, the plan soon firmed up into wanting to stay in England and marry her. What little information was coming out of Rumania and what I eventually learnt had happened to my sisters was not exactly positive. They had been taken to labour camps in Ukraine against their will and left me with even bigger doubts about returning to communist-led Rumania. In the end this just fuelled my dream of having my own family in England and then for us all to be re-united with my

German family sometime in the future.

I was so grateful for the kindness that had been shown to me by the local farmer to whom I had been assigned from the camp, and to the local man, Mr. Rich, who by his generosity had brought Flo and I together. On discharge from the camp the farmer found me a job at another farm and this came with a small cottage. It was located in the picture-postcard Woolley Village which was about two miles from the camp. From there it was a similar distance to the local pit at Woolley Colliery. There was a 14th century church at the centre of the village, a community hall and just a few pretty stone cottages. The farm cottage which went with the job was a small terraced house in the centre of the village with a tiny garden at the back.

Once I began to settle in my new surroundings, I tried my best to prove to the local people that not all Germans were bad. I decided that the best way to make friends was to learn some fundamentals about the local passion for cricket and football and to avoid talking about politics, religion and the royal family. Perhaps an arbitrary choice, but it seemed to work. The locals loved their sports and though I went to watch the local cricket team, initially I had little understanding about what was going on. I couldn't work out why there were so many people on the pitch, but so few were running. I was much more at home in the pub talking about football.

I still felt a great sense of embarrassment at being part of the German army in earlier times and somehow felt I needed to justify myself. In my heart my allegiance remained towards Siebenburgen and not to Germany, but an experience in the camp just before we were discharged still haunted me. We prisoners had been gathered together and compelled to watch a Pathe News film about the discoveries made in Belsen and other concentration camps. I can truly say that we were all filled with disgust and horror at the images we saw and these will haunt me for the rest of my life.

Just after moving into the cottage I remember receiving my first letter from Hans who by now had left England. When he had been released, he had returned to Germany because of Sophie and the young son he had never seen. His plan was that some-day he could be re-united with his family. I was terribly shocked by the content of his first letter:

"*My dearest friend Johann,*

Well, old pal, against all the odds I have finally made it to Germany. Can you remember when we pledged to try to get to Bavaria if we survived the war? Guess what? I've made it, and am now living in a place called Gersthofen. It is a real pity that you are not here with me, but I understand your reasons for staying, you lucky boy. I would have done the same given the circumstances.

I have found some digs and a job in the town, which is close to the city of Augsburg. You could never guess just how very beautiful this city is. Somehow it has managed to remain intact and not been razed to the ground like nearby Nuremberg and Warzburg. It has a past going back to Roman times and lots of historic buildings and pretty squares and fountains.

The local people have been kind to me here and have helped me to settle. I wrote to my parents in Maldorf to see if they could forward a letter that I had written to Sophie. I haven't any idea which camp she was sent to but maybe they can find out back home and send my letter on. I also wrote a letter to my young son Freddie saying that I would do everything I could to get him and his mum to come and join me here.

You are probably already aware of this, but just in case, I thought I would say that the Russians have taken control of Rumania and they seem to be taking it out on the local community in Maldorf. What a cruel thing to do to send all our young people, men and women, to labour camps in Ukraine and Siberia. I understand that Sophie, Sara and Maria were taken away. How dreadful for them. I can't take in what Sophie must be feeling having to leave our poor Freddie behind. I dread to think what they must be experiencing and I curse the Russians for their cruelty. I am also devastated that my sister Katherina has also been taken, and I hope that she can remain with your sisters. They have always done their best to help her.

I feel so angry about this and helpless too. I just wish there was somebody there in authority who I could punch, but there is nothing any of us can do. I understand also that the houses of all Saxon families have been taken by the authorities and handed over to local Rumanians. My own family is only allowed to stay in part of the property and is having to pay rent to these people for the privilege of living in their own homes and tending their own fields and animals. I'm not sure how this has affected your family but I guess they may have suffered the same fate.

Freddie has been left in the care of his grandparents. I'm sure that he will be well looked after but I wonder whether I shall ever get to see either of them again. Promise me that you will write and let me know how you are getting on and please make your news a bit more promising than mine.

Hans.

Having received the letter from Hans I was undecided what to put in my reply, given the contrast in our fortunes. However, I did in fact send it, taking account of his new circumstances:

"Dear Hans,

Well done for making it to Bavaria. One up on me then in terms of our promise! I was so glad to hear that you made it safely to Germany and am chuffed that you are beginning to settle in. I will pray for things to get better and am sure it will eventually turn out ok for you. Life can be really shitty when it wants to be. I know just how you must be feeling about being separated from Sophie, Freddie and Katherina. I have the same feelings of sadness knowing what has happened to my sisters. All we can both do is try to think positively and pray for the best. I'm sure it will turn out right in the end. Perhaps you will hear soon from Sophie when she gets your letter. Hopefully she will be able to reassure you about the future. Let's hope that our young people are not needed for long in Ukraine and that their conditions are ok and they can return soon.

Here in England, I have also settled in a new village after being discharged from the camp. As you know, I met up with a local girl and we plan to marry in the future once I have secured a better job and am more accepted by the locals. Flo is a bit like your Sophie. Nice looking, good-tempered, and very patient. Like Sophie, she's also a great cook. I enjoy working on the farm but the pay is poor and I need to earn more if I am to get married and support her. Her father is a great guy and is trying to get me a job down the local coal mine, which pays much better. Ok, it's a dangerous job, but it opens up the chance for us to get a pit property in the village there and for me to earn good money.

The locals aren't too bad, but I am trying to keep a low profile particularly as I have snatched the prettiest girl in the village from under their noses. I'll try to find out at this end what is happening in Rumania and Ukraine and let you have any information I can find. There is a guy here who was our translator in the camp and has been helpful and he might be able to get more information. Please, keep in touch.

Johann.

In my time off from the new job I used to walk down through Woolley woods to meet up with Flo. She and her family lived in nearby Woolley Colliery village. Sometimes, as I got to the outskirts of the village, some of the local youths would have a go at me;

- You Gerry bastard, piss off home and leave our girls alone. We don't want your scum here, so bugger off.

Initially I used to rise to the bait and shout insults back at them, but this is exactly what they were after. I soon learnt that the best tactic was to ignore the jibes and eventually they got fed up of trying to rile me. After a few months I was lucky to get an opportunity to work down the pit, thanks to the efforts of Flo's Dad. With the offer of a job came the prospect of a house in the pit village itself, so this was something to look forward to. It was not such a pretty place as Woolley itself, just four rows of terraced houses backing on to the pit. After a while I had become known as 'Johnny' to Flo's parents and eventually the name stuck.

Once I got the job at the pit, after a period of intensive training, I moved in to stay initially with Flo and her parents. We slept in separate rooms of course and we both accepted this without question as it was very much in keeping with the values of her parents and local expectations. They were so kind to us and helped us plan our wedding. Living in the village had been great from the point of view of access to work, plus I had gradually become better known locally and to those who worked with me down the pit. It was a bit strange that there were no street names in the village. You could see the great wheel of the pit-head machinery from the back garden, and the vista of lush green fields stretching in the opposite direction. Across the street from the house was a fish and chip shop, which the locals used a lot. Having had my first sample of these, I could see why. On the next street up there was a small grocer's shop on the corner, where the locals got what goods they could, as many things at that time were still in short supply.

Most of the village-based miners quickly got to know me and were welcoming eventually. It didn't happen overnight, but because I took a low-profile approach when I was out and about the locals came to accept me. It was also down to their basic friendliness in the end and I soon came to realise how the families in this part of the world were basically very kind and supportive of each other. I also took to this because it reminded me of how we used to live in Maldorf.

However, one or two of the outside workers who travelled each day on the pit buses to their work, were less forgiving and were quick to make their resentment known to me. As an example, shortly after starting at the pit some idiot had shouted at me as he got off the bus:

- Hey Fritz, what do you think you are doing coming over here and taking our jobs and our women. Why don't you just fuck off home?

Delivered as it was in a strong Yorkshire accent this sounded much less threatening to me, and quite comical. In any case, by then I had developed a thick skin and had learnt to rise above it. I had also learnt from my friends that a swift gesture with two fingers did the job.

Chapter Seven

June 1947 - Pit-Head baths

I thought I had learnt to ride with the occasional jibes, but on one occasion I let myself down. At least that was how I thought of it at the time, as I had taken great pride in not rising to the ignorant comments of a few. I was coming off a hard eight-hour shift at the coalface. The work at the pit-face was really hard. The conditions were horrific, working on a small narrow seam, in sweltering heat. Initially it had felt claustrophobic and all you could think about was the tons of rock overhead held up by the props that had been driven in as the seam advanced. Eventually though you just concentrated on the job in hand, chipping away to reveal the coal.

On this occasion the lift clanked open as usual and we all spilled out and collectively breathed in the fresh air. The sense of relief getting to the surface was hard to describe. It must be how fish feel when they break the surface to breathe. We were all jet black from head to foot, covered in coal dust. Exhausted, we headed for the baths. I felt a sense of bliss shaking off the grimy clothes and headed naked to the showers. The work down the pit was hard and strenuous and had etched all of our bodies into quite trim and muscular frames. We were almost as sleek as athletes and footballers. To an outsider I guess it would have struck an impressive, if grubby, picture as we entered the showers.

I remember that as I was leaving the shower the next shift

of outside workers was entering the changing rooms and one of them, seeing me, took my clothes and threw them into the wet shower floor next to me before I had chance to stop him. At this point I just lost my rag. It wasn't like me to get angry like that, but I guess all the pent-up feelings that I must have been holding back over the previous months, trying not to rise to the baiting, had finally got to me. The others around me were stunned by my reaction, as I was normally such a placid person.

The guy who had thrown the clothes then shouted:

- Why didn't you stay at home and screw your own women instead of coming over here to shag ours? You bastards started the war and now you think you can just stay and take our jobs. Who the hell do you think you are?

I didn't take time out to answer this time, I just saw stars and exploded into action. My first punch floored the biggest of them and then his mate came flying towards me. It must have been a bit of a comic scene seeing me throwing punches in the buff, standing there defiantly. I remember being flung backwards into the shower area but I was able to grab my attacker and had the better of him, until the original guy came back and kicked me hard, so that I released my hold.

By now I was beginning to realise I was in trouble trying to take the two of them on, but thankfully my mate Billy had heard the commotion and joined in. He took hold of the smaller guy leaving me to grapple with the other one. He decided to up the stakes by insulting Flo and questioning my parentage, but this just spurred me on. Then I got lucky. My adversary swung a massive punch at me, but thankfully he missed and slipped on the floor. As he got up, I landed a solid blow on his chin and he fell backwards, cracking his head on the floor.

As his blood flowed gently across the floor and into the shower drain, Billy shouted:

-   Now piss off and pick a fight somewhere else. Johnny's our mate and one of us.

We knew at that point that they wouldn't tangle with the two of us again and true enough, when he had picked himself up off the floor, he and his mate sidled off throwing lame curses back at us as they left.

Later that evening, in the Miners Welfare, Billy was in his element, pint in hand, spouting off to our mates at the bar.

-   Bloody hell you should have seen Johnny earlier in the baths. God he just flew into this guy and his mate. I didn't know he had it in him. I tell you they won't be messing with him again.

Incredulously someone chipped in:

-   No way. I don't believe you. Johnny's the quietest guy I know. Wouldn't hurt a fly! Good on you mate.

Looking back, I got lucky I think, but from that day forward the insults stopped at work. Over time in the Miner's Welfare this incident would often be the source of much hilarity amongst me and my village pals. Each time in the telling of the story the number of fellas that I beat up got bigger and the damage inflicted got worse!

Joe Louis, watch out!

Chapter Eight

August 1947

Shortly after this incident, as I was about to meet up with Flo, she came running towards me excitedly. Previously we had been talking about the future together and I sensed something was up.

- Look at this Johnny, I can't believe it.

She was waving a copy of the Barnsley Chronicle at me and showed me the article that had clearly excited her. Of course, my English was still very ropey, so I asked her to read it out to me. She read the headline first:

German PoW marries English woman: Southampton Shocked.

Then she read out the rest of the article.

Heinz Fellbrich, a German PoW, and his new wife June (nee Till) were married on the 14th August 1947 at a quiet service at Southampton Registry Office. Heinz is the first German PoW to wed an English woman since such marriages were legalised last month. There has been a mixed response to the event with June reporting that some people have spat at her whilst out walking.

Immediately after the ceremony Heinz was returned to his camp where he remains until further notice.

Flo had been closely following the reports of the fierce

debates in parliament about the rights and wrongs of women being allowed to marry German prisoners. It had got to that stage because of one case in particular where a judgement had been made, which then became law, that if such a marriage took place the woman would lose her British citizenship. As a consequence, we had been very cautious about how we behaved in public and hadn't felt confident in planning our future. I certainly didn't want to risk Flo's legal status. Thankfully, this had caused a furore and a backlash of public sympathy across the nation which began to influence the political debate.

Just a few days earlier Flo had read an account in the Daily Mirror of the official Hansard record for the 8th August 1947 and relayed this to me:

Mrs Leagh Manning asked the Secretary of State for War why his Department exercises sexual discrimination against English women wishing to marry German Prisoners of War, when no such embargo exists on marriages between British serving men and German girls.

The newspaper article had then quoted the reply in Hansard from Secretary of State Bellings:

Prisoner of War regulations have hitherto forbidden prisoners to have sexual relations with British women. These regulations will now be amended

Flo went on reading out the rest of the article about the Southampton couple and it truly was a remarkable story.

Heinz had apparently seen her looking into the camp through the chain link fence and the two of them had begun to talk to each other and then struck up a relationship in this strange way. Both described this as love at first sight. I could relate to this in the way I had been immediately struck by Flo when I saw her across the dance floor. The story got even more dramatic as Heinz had then apparently tunnelled out of the camp under the cover of night to meet her. So here it was, just the sign that we had been waiting for. This was like a red light for us to go ahead.

- *Come on Johnny, what are we waiting for? God, if they can do that, why can't we?*

We later learnt that we were not alone in being inspired by their story as there were to be many subsequent applications to marry across the country. Within days we had plucked up the courage to finally approach Flo's parents to get their blessing. I had felt so lucky at the time when she accepted my offer of marriage. The local vernacular here would have been that I had "dropped on". I was so pleased when her father gave his permission.

Somehow, though, I still felt a little bit guilty about my situation. I guess it was because I realised just how much I had gained and how much Hans by contrast had lost, given his separation from Sophie and Freddie. I worried about how he must have struggled in his first few months in the camp in Cumbria and how his choice after the war was so much more difficult than mine. He had no reason to stay in England, but the prospect of going back to Rumania was off the agenda since the Russians had taken control there and the news of how they were using their power back home was poor. He must have felt that he had no option but to take up the offer of repatriation to Germany. Nevertheless, he was bound to have doubts about this as despite the German heritage he would have no idea what life in Germany would hold. Also he must have felt isolated as he would remain separated from his family.

In a strange way events had taken a cruel twist for him. In the beginning of all this we shared something of the same bitterness at being dragged into the war together and the same grief at what had happened to our loved ones back home at the end of the war. Yes, I still worried about what was happening to my sisters but I had got Flo in compensation. He was still grieving about what had happened to Katherina and all he could do was to worry about Sophie and Freddie without any certainty for the future.

I also thanked my good luck that I had quickly come to love Yorkshire and its people. I loved its grittiness and the natural beauty of the countryside, sitting comfortably alongside the industrial landmarks of the pits. Although the locals had taken some time to warm to me, once I was accepted, I had found that the local people would do absolutely anything to help. I felt so lucky to have been sent to Yorkshire to do my camp service. I quickly came to appreciate why the locals called it "God's own country" here.

January 1948 – Darton village

Flo's parents were brilliant about my wedding proposal and immediately set about supporting us in our plans. The local vicar at All Saints church in the nearby village of Darton was happy to perform the ceremony and we got married on the 15th May 1948. Afterwards, although we couldn't afford a big do, the reception in the Miners Welfare was lovely, and Walt stood a couple of rounds for the small number of guests who had been invited. Not bad for a Yorkshireman, I thought, having laughed initially when my pals had told me about the joke regarding their supposed meanness.

My ambitions for the future went up a gear six months later when Flo told me she was pregnant. I decided that I would take every bit of overtime offered and save like mad for our child-to-be. We had been in the queue for a house in Woolley Colliery village, which is immediately next to the pit. Shortly afterwards the good news came through that we had a home of our own.

Chapter Nine

December, 1953

The job continued to go well and little Johnny flourished growing up in the village. As a small child he had the benefit of his mother's total care. We had decided that Flo had enough on her plate looking after him, managing the running of the home and tending our chickens and thriving vegetable plot. This wasn't out of the norm in Woolley Colliery village as most of the women were housewives and didn't have a separate job. We had the benefit of Flo's parents living locally and occasionally they would baby-sit and allow us a night out at the Welfare. It was nice occasionally to go out together and I would sit contentedly with my pint and Flo would sip her Wicked Lady cocktail. Just a bit of luxury once in a while and it made her feel a bit special.

There were other toddlers living nearby and so Johnny had a few playmates and could be left to play safely either in our garden or that of a neighbour's. Once a year we got away on a week's holiday to Bridlington with Flo's parents. They had been going there for years and went to the same boarding house in Marshall Avenue. Walt would take me off to the promenade each morning and attempt to show me how to play crown green bowls. I never quite got used to the different bias on either side of the bowls, and was in awe at Walt's prowess and how he could get his bowls to settle by the jack. There were bowling greens all along the promenade so we were spoilt for choice. Most times we would catch a crafty pint at the Windsor pub on the way home. Walt had been coming there each year for a long time and was well known by the regulars.

In the afternoon I would take Johnny down to the beach and find a nice spot dependant on the tides. There was such a lot to do for children and we never tired of these trips to the seaside. Looking back on Johnny's early years I remember how nervous we had been when it came to the time when he had to start school. Given his birth date at the end of August he was the youngest in his intake and we worried how he would fare against the other slightly older children. The first day was hell and we had trouble getting him to stay, plus there were tears. He did settle though quite quickly and it was good to watch him flourish in the school environment. Flo loved to read to him and talk about the day's events at school.

As I got more settled at work and started to earn better wages, I was determined to save up so that I could take the family to Germany to meet up with Hans and Sophie and the rest of the family. We had been corresponding regularly and Hans was insistent that we come to see them. Not that I took much persuading. It took me a lot of extra shifts to get the savings to afford the visit, but over a lengthy period of time I had enough to go ahead.

I remember how excited I was walking into Barnsley town centre to book the flight to Germany but I wasn't exactly sure where the travel shop was. Somebody had told me it was near to Peel Street but that was as far as it went. I hadn't told Flo about my visit to Barnsley as I thought that she had enough on her plate bringing up a youngster and looking after the house. I hoped she would like the idea of a trip to Germany but I wanted to get the details sorted first.

My earnings down the pit had been good, but without the extra work it would have been a struggle to be able to plan a foreign trip. One expense I had to factor in was that as a Yorkshire miner I was expected to go out with the lads at the end of the week for a few pints. Not that this had been a great compromise. In fact, it had been a bonus for me in terms of getting accepted as one of the lads. Nevertheless, it had placed a bit of a strain on the budget. I had been surprised initially at how much these boys could put away. Before I had come to England, I thought that we could drink back home in Maldorf, but this had been on a different scale. When Billy had taken me under his wing, I remember his famous words:

-    Eight or nine pints, lad, or you're not a proper bloke! Gerrit darn yer, it'll do yer good.

I enjoyed the camaraderie, and to be truthful, come Friday each week I was so knackered that the thought of a few pints with my mates was something to look forward to. It didn't weaken my resolve though to take Flo and little Johnny to see my family in South Germany and I always

78

made sure that I had money to put away each week before I handed over my wages to Flo. Luckily, Flo and her parents had been very supportive of my social life and I was grateful for that. I am sure they recognised that I wasn't like some of the lads who could get violent in drink and take it out on their wives or girlfriends.

As time moved on, Hans' letters had become much more pleasant to read as he had now settled and been reunited with Sophie. The only element of sadness had been the news that his sister Katherina had died in unfortunate circumstances in the labour camp. It was difficult to comprehend the dreadful circumstances she had found in the camp and the pain that she and my sisters must have felt. Hans had reflected on this when he wrote initially but he clearly had moved on, especially since he and Sophie had been reunited. He wrote positively about his new surroundings. From Hans' description, the city of Augsburg, which was just north of Munich in Bavaria, sounded like it would be well worth a visit in any case. However, the main attraction was to meet up with family and show our little Johnny a different aspect of life. It was good that Hans and I had been allowed the occasional letter when we were prisoners and had managed to keep in touch throughout our period in the camps. His return to Germany and reunion with Sophie had been re-assuring. A lot of water had gone under the bridge since the end of the war, but his letters had given me a glimpse into how life in Germany after the war had developed. I had no real concept of what a German city would be like. Although I had grown up as part of a German community in Rumania, I had never thought of going to Germany in those days. We had all been very content with village life, with the occasional trip to the local town of Hermannstadt. But that didn't compare with what we were to experience in Germany. I was dying to see how it compared to Barnsley.

Hans had told me in his more recent letters that he had finally been able to afford to build a property in Gersthofen, near to Augsburg. He had told me a bit about how Sophie and Sara had managed to escape from their horrors in Ukraine and had found their way to Bavaria, but their story seemed too fantastical to be true. Nevertheless, I longed for the opportunity to meet them again and to hear about their experiences in person.

My elder sister Maria had also been in a labour camp but she had been sent to Siberia. Unlike her sisters, after her release, she had then been transported back to Rumania and had re-settled in Maldorf. I didn't know the details of her story, but from what Hans told me, in the early days of her return to Maldorf, she helped to look after Freddie until eventually the family were able to wade through the bureaucracy of post war Rumania and succeeded in getting the papers to release him back to his parents in Germany.

Once I found the travel shop in Barnsley, I had no idea what to expect. I remember that when I walked in and spoke with the young man behind the desk, he had a look of utter shock. There I was with my slightly dodgy Yorkshire - cum - German accent. Also, I guess he didn't have much call for arranging flights to Germany given the recent past. However, once I had shown him my bank book, with the necessary savings clearly marked, he could see that he had a bona-fide customer and he then got on with the job of sorting out options. It turned out that the only flights available and affordable within my budget were to Dusseldorf in the north of Germany. It would have been preferable to fly to Munich in the south, but it was much dearer to go via there and we would have had to get a flight from London Airport. He told me that from Dusseldorf we could catch a train to Augsburg and then on to Gersthofen. I was so happy and agreed some dates during the school holidays and put down a deposit as required by the agent.

I needn't have worried at what Flo would think of what I had done, because when I told her she was so happy. I realised that this would be the first time she or any of her family had been out of the country, let alone flown in an aeroplane. In the weeks following this young Johnny couldn't stop talking about it with his new school friends. Once I had told him about the planned visit, he took to looking for pictures of aircraft at every juncture. He was so open to new experiences. I remember how excited he had been the first time he saw the young trainee miners coming up the street covered in coaldust. There he had been, playing in the front yard, when the line of face-blackened teenagers passed the gate in their blue overalls and orange hats. In earlier days they would have been more of a mixed bunch of trainees known as Bevin boys. I had been fascinated by the stories my mates told me about the Bevin boy era, most of which had been passed down from their dads. Just after the war had started the Minister had created a scheme to recruit people to work in the mines, where there was a shortage of labour to produce the quantity of coal needed to feed the munitions industry. One in five of the male population who were not otherwise engaged in fighting duties or specialised occupations, were balloted into the mines. They came from different backgrounds and met with some derision from some in the population who would call them draft-dodgers or worse. They had also been met with opposition from the main mining workforce who feared their jobs might be threatened.

Now though, in calmer times, the trainees were drawn from their local communities and well respected. As Johnny peered over the gate this time, they were on their way home to the tin bath laid out by their mother in front of the coal fire. Unlike their older colleagues they weren't allowed the luxury of the pit head baths! He couldn't tear his eyes away from the parade of blackened would-be miners.

Just before we were due to fly, we had a wonderful afternoon at the annual village fair. This was held on the open fields opposite the Welfare. There was a carnival atmosphere and the sun was shining brightly. Amongst the stalls and usual attractions, preparations were taking place for one of the major features of the day. The miners rescue team was rehearsing their procedures in front of a large crowd in the miner's welfare sports ground. They had recreated the cramped conditions of the mine shaft, by means of a long and low wooden open framework. They had to crawl through this in their teams at no more than waist height whilst unravelling the many metres of hosepipe behind them.

Two teams at a time competed alongside each other to see who could do this in the best time and this was obviously brilliant practise for the eventuality of a fire underground. We joined in watching as part of the big crowd from our village and beyond. The joy from the event was so obvious with kids watching the events, eating ice cream and crisps, and all thoroughly amazed at the dexterity of the miners. It also provided some of the parents with an opportunity to sneak off for a crafty drink in the Welfare, whilst the children tucked into their goodies and watched the show.

Chapter Ten

August 1954 - Dusseldorf, North Germany

When we set off for Germany, a neighbour, Bill Travis, drove us over to Ringway airport near Manchester. As we waited in the Terminal building, Johnny was so excited seeing the blue and white livery of the Vickers Viscount aircraft. As we walked across the runway to get on board, he couldn't get over the shiny rotating propellers and the sleek metallic livery of the plane.

Once we had arrived at the airport in Dusseldorf, we headed for the railway station. The sounds and the smells on the way were so different from England. We were all hungry and we were drawn in by the strong aroma of the local sausage and frankfurters being served on the stalls on the roadside. This must have seemed strange fare to a near five-year old from Yorkshire. There was no sign of sausage rolls or pork pies, but Johnny's eyes lit up at the sight of the largest sausage that he had ever seen, now wrapped up in a giant bread roll. I had to buy it for him just to see how he would take to frankfurters. I was not disappointed as he tucked into his treat with gusto. His pleasure was indescribable and he seemed immediately to be at one with his new environment. Through this gastronomic treat he had discovered his German heritage.

Five hours later Sophie and Hans met us on the station platform in Gersthofen. Sophie and I were so overwhelmed at seeing each other that we both broke down in tears and hugged each other tightly. Hans was waiting next to her on the platform. It had been some ten years since we had last met, so this was also a very emotional moment for us. I remember that Johnny looked bemused as we two grown men hugged each other and broke down into tears. He must have thought how un-Yorkshire-like this was, before being suddenly swept up in the arms of his new family members.

It took us just ten minutes to walk to their house in Peter-Dorfler Street. They lived in the downstairs accommodation and above them was another family who, like themselves, had originated from Rumania. We came to know the Zikeli family well during our stay. They told us that they were also from Maldorf and they had their own interesting story to tell about the war years. They told us that their son Horst had been Freddie's best friend back in Maldorf.

I found it remarkable to hear how these ex-Rumanian families had come to support each other after the war. From Hans' description of what he had found when he had first arrived, it was clear that post-war Germany had emerged badly from the devastation of conflict. The state had been able to afford very little help to these families who were being re-patriated. Also, there had been some resentment from the indigenous residents towards these "foreign" families suddenly arriving into their once settled communities. I learnt over the next couple of days that in these circumstances each returning Rumanian family had joined together to support each other, to help find jobs and provide practical and emotional support when needed. In the Flagner and Zikeli case this had gone as far as pooling their savings to build their own house together. One family downstairs and the other above.

During our stay we were dazzled by the sights that we saw, which were unimaginable. On our first visit to Augsburg, we found a truly memorable city which had somehow escaped the worst excesses of the bombing during the war. It's main thoroughfare, Maximilian Strasse, had a number of ornate Mercury fountains and at its head a beautiful cathedral known locally as the Dom. Further down Maximilian Strasse on another day we spent some time in the Rathaus, the town hall of the city. It was built in the early part of the seventeenth century in true Renaissance style. Despite severe damage during the war the external appearance and splendour of the building remained. Inside however, the damage to the Goldener Saal, or Golden Hall, had been extensive and the original gilding that had adorned the surfaces had been largely lost. There were illustrations and photographs as to how the Hall had looked before and there were plans eventually to return the gilding to its original state. It was situated on the second floor. The room was immense covering over five hundred square metres and had a ceiling height of nearly fifty feet. All around the walls and on the ceiling had once been beautiful paintings and murals depicting religious scenes. In its prime this room must have rivalled the Sistine

Chapel. Now many of these masterpieces had been damaged and awaited future renovation.

Also, there were so many miles of narrow canals running through the city that the locals claimed it to be more prolific than Venice. Everywhere we went, these waterways showed their face and the city's Roman history peeped out onto its majestic streets. Strangely, it was the Fuggerei district which most captured my heart. Apparently in medieval times the rich Fugger family had funded many projects for royalty and dynasties across Europe. What was most impressive was that they also had the vision and compassion to build a whole village of alms houses for the poor and under -privileged sections of the community. The place had narrow streets and tiny houses, each with its own shaped door handle to help the tenant identify their place at night time as there were no street lights. The tenants only paid a minimal peppercorn rent, equivalent to the original amount of one Rhenish guilder which was equivalent to about two Deutschmark. In addition, they had to be Catholic, have a low income and no debt. In the past, if the residents missed the ten pm curfew deadline they were fined, but we were told that things were a little more relaxed now.

We spent much of the rest of this visit meeting other friends and family members. This included George who was Hans' brother and of course my sister Sara. On one of the days, we met up with her and her daughter Rosalinde at the Tiergarten which was the city zoo. Sara insisted on buying ice-cream for the children and a Weissbier for myself in the beer garden, whilst she and Flo drank coffee. I know that she didn't have a lot of money at her disposal, but she was so generous and clearly took great satisfaction from sharing what she had. The week's visit had gone so quickly and we determined that we would return as soon as possible. Sophie and Flo were like sisters throughout the visit and despite the language barrier, they got on so well. Flo was fascinated by the meals that Sophie cooked for us, which were very traditional Siebenburgen dishes. Other than the trips in Augsburg, we found during the stay that we didn't need to go too far for enjoyment, and we spent the remainder of our time walking in the nearby forests and fields.

Chapter Eleven

July 1956 - Gersthofen

It was in fact just less than two years before we visited again. When we had returned after the first visit Johnny had nagged me incessantly about going back. I had done very much the same as last time by working extra shifts and saving like mad. Some of the savings had to go to improving our house, but this took a back seat generally in terms of allocating our monies. Florrie was good also in that she wasn't bothered about fancy clothes and new-fangled bits of furniture. I never thought about how she dressed anyway because she just looked lovely and could have worn anything as far as I was concerned.

During this stay we had our first introduction to 'Uncle' Burtz. He wasn't really a direct relative but had become part of the extended family and made an immediate impression on Johnny. He took great pride in taking bites out of raw onions and chillies. Despite my warning, Johnny tried a bit of chilli and immediately regretted it! Sophie was not amused and gave Burtz an almighty telling off.

Wherever we visited we sat and chatted and took the food and drinks which were always so kindly provided. The men would drink the local beer with a shot of home-made schnapps, while the women took tea or coffee with a large piece of cake. It could be a little difficult for Flo and Johnny, given the language differences, but they were very patient and could see the friendship and generosity for what it was. On one visit we were taken to see an older man who had managed to leave Maldorf after the war, just before it had become difficult to get out under communist rule. He was a former friend of Hans' father and took great pride in showing us around his garden. He was growing his own vegetables and capturing rainwater in a number of tubs and receptacles. There were chickens roaming everywhere and toys lay around where his grandchildren would play when they came to visit. It reminded me a lot of the sort of gardens we used to have in Rumania. It was a lovely outdoor space with some nice shady areas under the trees.

As we sat down to take our drinks Johnny shouted out and pointed to something hanging from one of the trees. The old man laughed and went to the tree and pulled down a large salami from the lower branch. We had of course by now started into his home-made schnapps but even before he carved us a slice to try with some bread, I could smell that it had been maturing for some time. In my earlier days I had got used to this type of home-made salami but now even to my palate the salami was well past its best and very difficult to eat. Nevertheless, politeness dictated that we finish what he had given. I made as if it was delicious and asked if I could have a beer to wash it down. Johnny did his best but when the man wasn't looking, I saw him feeding the meat to a passing chicken. We left knowing that the kind old man was happy in his mind that we appreciated his home produced wurst!

It was events like this that left an indelible feeling of belonging, and sense of pride at being alongside these very generous and welcoming people from my homeland. We would be definitely returning. There was no doubt about that. I resolved that I would make this happen quicker next time and take on as many extra shifts as I could.

Chapter Twelve

February 15th 1958

Woolley Colliery village was awoken at 8 am by the noise that everyone in the place had come to dread. It didn't happen very often, and most of the younger generation hadn't heard it before, but that ear-shattering sound had been described through each generation of miners and their families. It was a mighty blast from the pit whistle that broke the silence today. There was no doubting what it was, and across the village, on each of the long terraces of houses, people rushed out onto the street and glanced across to the pit, hoping for the best but fearing the worst.

February 22nd 1958 – Inquest hearing, Barnsley

George Ogden, a coal filler at Woolley Colliery pit, was called to give evidence at the Inquest as he was working near to Johann Winkler on the 17th February. He was the first person to find his colleague after hearing a loud noise and then his own name being shouted out. George explained that he considered that they had been working on a dangerous seam without the roof being properly supported. He said that the roof was cracked on both sides, in a bad condition and that this had been previously reported to the authorities. He went on to say that after he heard a shout of "George", he dropped his shovel and went to find Johann. When he got to him, Johann, or Johnny as they called him locally, was covered by an eleven-foot slab of stone, with only his head and left shoulder visible. He said that it took fifteen minutes to extricate him from the rock and that he was in an unconscious state. It looked as if Johnny had been trying to jump aside to avoid the fall, but was hit by what was estimated as a two-ton rockfall.

A further witness, Colin Farnsworth, the deputy on the shift, said that he had examined the accident site and didn't think that the seam was properly supported in that area. He said that there had been reports to this effect sent to the NCB Health and Safety department, but that they had received no reply.

The representative of the National Coal Board gave evidence also and expressed their condolences to the family. He stressed the excellent track record of accidents within the mining industry over a ten-year period and the fact that they could find no evidence of any negative reports relating to this particular seam. The representative said that it was the intention of the NCB to offer compensation to the family as the deceased left behind a widow and two young children.

The coroner gave his verdict of accidental death after hearing the evidence.

February 28th 1958

Barnsley Chronicle headline: "Freak fall kills ex POW"

A tragic accident occurred at Woolley Colliery pit on the 15th of

February, causing the death of Johann Winkler, a popular ex POW, who had stayed on after the war and married a local girl. An NUM official said that the miner would be greatly missed, but emphasised that this was a freak accident, the first of its sort in 10 years of safe working on this particular coal face. A colleague informed us that Johann did not normally work Saturdays, but he was apparently doing overtime to save for a further trip to Germany with his young family, which was planned in a fortnights time.

In the obituary section:

WINKLER, Johnny Beloved husband and daddy, accidentally killed at Woolley Colliery, aged 36 years.

I cannot hear your voice,

Or take your hand in mine,

But none can rob me of my dreams,

Or steal your heart away.

Time heals they say, perhaps it does,

But memory clings and so does love.

From his loving wife Flo.

A loving son to help and aid,

One who was better God never made.

A wonderful worker, loyal and true,

One in a million, dear Son were you.

From Mam and Dad Birkinshaw and Gilbert.

Funeral – All Saints Church, Darton

Early March 1958

Jack Teague, a local Deputy, says a few words at the funeral on behalf of Johann's colleagues:

- *John Winkler was a former German POW who was held at a camp at the far end of Woolley Edge during the Second World War. He was one hell of a nice man, and I don't think I can remember anyone having anything bad to say about him. He was a brave man to decide to stay in England, knowing just how much hostility there would be to a German living here. I have always had a great admiration for him and I am sure so did a lot of other people."*

Outside the weather is warm and sunny and afterwards a small crowd gathers in the graveyard. The parish vicar says a few final words and consoles Flo, who is flanked by her parents. Her eight-year-old son holds his mother's hand and a pram stands close by with his baby brother of just over three months inside. Flo is full of grief and has not yet had time to think about the stark realities which lie ahead. Being a single parent and having to look after two young children will undoubtedly mean years of having to rely on benefits and trying to make ends meet. As compensation for the accident, the NCB has left a sum of £1000 for each child, held in Trust until their eighteenth birthdays.

Several of the young miners in attendance come over to the widow to pay their respects. It is clear to her that they have great respect for Johnny as they knew him and each find their own words to express this.

A few hours later in the miner's welfare the funeral party and a large number of his work colleagues gather to pay their respects to Johnny, a young man and father who has been so tragically killed in an accident at the local pit. The family hadn't the resources to throw a fancy wake, but his work colleagues had chipped in to support the small bash at the welfare.

Flo tries desperately to hold back the tears as she trudges back to her terraced cottage in the nearby pit village. On the table in the kitchen are the many letters of condolence she has received from families in the village. Theirs is a close- knit community and although she knows there are people that she can turn to, deep down she is at a loss as to how she is going to cope in the future.

Footnote:

Report of HM Inspectors of Mines for 1958:

It is pleasing to report that in 1958 the total of 43 persons killed is 22 less than for 1957. (This was) ... the lowest ever recorded. For the first time in any one year the number of persons killed underground was less than 40.

There were 4 face-working fall deaths against a yearly average of 10.3

Part 2

Sophie and Sara

Sophie and Sara, June 1944

SOPHIE

Chapter One

1930 – 1938

Looking back to my early childhood years it is strange to think that despite what was to come this time still evokes such happy memories. People I talked with in later life would say that I must have been aware of the impending war and the troubles that were brewing in Germany. The truth was that we had always been brought up to think of ourselves as Saxons first and Siebenburgen by nationality. True enough, at school we were taught about the region's ancient German heritage, and we fervently held on to traditions that went back several centuries. However, the turmoil that I later learnt about relating to pre-Nazi-Germany was not taught in school and none of it discussed in the village until much later.

What I do remember from those early days back in Rumania was a childhood filled with great joy. Altogether there were four children in our family. Maria was the oldest, then came Johann, followed by myself and finally Sara the youngest. I was very close to my sister Sara, despite our different characters and temperaments. Being a few years older, Maria had her own circle of friends and tended to spend her free time with them. Sara would be the first to admit that I was very much the sensible one between us. By contrast she was unpredictable, fearless and a real firebrand who lived on her instincts. Of course, Johann was special to all of us being the only boy and having the most wonderful disposition. He was slim, handsome and kind and much admired by his peers in the village.

One thing was certain, it didn't take much to get Sara excited and this would mean that at any one time she could be running around happily in unabandoned fashion or else in a fiery mood if something had upset or challenged her. She was fiercely protective if anyone dared to upset or threaten me. It was like having your own pocket-sized bodyguard with you at all times. I guess the people in the village saw her as a fire-brand, but no matter what, we in the family loved and cherished her. Safe to say, life around Sara provided no dull moments and although she would often get me into trouble with her antics, I always forgave her in the end.

To illustrate this, one incident in particular stands out which was to have great significance for the future. One day in the school playground we saw that a girl called Katherina was being surrounded by a group of children. Earlier in the classroom she had been too nervous to answer a simple question from the teacher and she was generally very shy and reserved. I dragged Sara with me to see what was happening and when we got there, we could see Katherina sobbing on the floor, surrounded by a posse of screaming girls who were hurling insults at her.

-   You stupid girl, why are you at our school, you
    should be at the special school.

- You are so dumb, maybe you should stay at home with your mum.

We knew that she was extremely shy in school but had never really appreciated her vulnerability before. We had some affinity to her only in the fact that she was the sister of Hans who was Johann's closest friend. Coincidentally he was the only boy in the village that I had a bit of a crush on. I didn't admit it at the time of course, but to me he always stood out as the bravest and most respected amongst the boys of our age.

When she realised that Katherina was being picked on Sara immediately saw red and jumped into the fray, shouting at the girls to back off. As usual I stood off and let her get on with it, but I feared that this could easily go wrong. First, she shielded Katherina with her body and then began to viciously spit out insults.

- Step back you idiots and leave her alone.
- Do that again and you are dead.
- Your mothers stink like fish.

This last comment was the ultimate insult and I feared it would spark a fight, but Sara's reputation went before her and they all backed off. I moved to put my arms around Katherina and the others just melted quietly away. Once again, they had learnt not to cross paths with Sara. This incident developed into a pact of protection towards Katherina between myself and Sara and served to cement what was to become a lasting friendship between us. In return Katherina repaid us many times over by giving us her undying gratitude and camaraderie.

Alongside these typical childhood incidents, growing up in Maldorf before the war had been a pleasure. Generally speaking, all of us as young children had shared the traditions that had passed down through the centuries and which placed a great emphasis on the importance of the position of children within the community. Just before Christmas we would go with our parents and teachers in groups into the forest to pick flowers and plants to tie to the Lichter. This would be displayed in the church as part of the festive celebrations and remain there until the sixth of January.

In early January the younger children, normally those who were not yet confirmed, would go from house to house giving their good wishes and receiving small amounts of money in return. This was followed in early February with a children's ball which was a dance at the church. When we were a little older, at Easter, we were encouraged to place a light and small Christmas tree in an upstairs window to encourage a boyfriend and placed flowers in the hat of the lucky chosen one. All the boys would get excited at this time of year and would be encouraged to go out at night time to search for the light. I wasn't one for chasing the boys but it gave me at an early stage an opportunity to show my admiration for Hans. I remember Sara getting excited about this on my behalf and encouraging me to do this. No doubt she wound up Johann and got him to tip off Hans.

Johann told me that he wanted to make sure that the trick would work and had urged Hans on:

- Come on Hans you know you want to do it. You've got to go out tonight and look for the light.

There were other traditions which the whole village joined in. On May 1st local musicians played in church followed by a dance later in the village hall. One special occasion was the Peter and Paul ceremony, where we all danced around three wheels of different sizes all decorated with flowers and with sweets and bottles of beer attached to the bottom wheel. This must sound strange to an outsider, but these were the traditions that had been passed down to us.

Our family lived in a grand old house which was well over a hundred years old. I imagine that in earlier times it had seen days of splendour because it had lovely big rooms with high ceilings and there were large gates at the front which opened out onto a spacious courtyard. There was a large garden at the rear of the house where my parents grew vegetables and fruit which provided the bulk of our daily needs throughout the year. They also owned land and forestry around the village. Here we kept animals and grew produce, together with earning additional monies from the forestry products, such as logs and fences, which we sold on to the community. The grain we grew went to the mill in the village which kept everyone supplied for their bread-making and baking. All in all, our family was self-sufficient and there were jobs for everyone within this operation for

103

all of us as children as we grew up.

I had tried to keep my feelings for Hans hidden from Sara and played the part like most girls of pretending to ignore the boys in the village. She was ahead of me on this though and pretty soon she made it clear that she knew how I felt. We used to bump into Hans a lot as he was our brother's closest friend. I tried to ignore him and the other boys when we were out and about, but I guess too that he sensed how I felt about him. On a typical day we would wake early, even before our parents had begun their daily chores, and meet with a few other girls in the village square. Our numbers never varied much but if we were joined by others, there were never more than six or seven of us.

We had grown up together in this beautiful community, living the idyllic childhood just as our parents had done and generations before them. Sometimes up in the fields and hills we would bump into the boys. Their activities were slightly more robust than ours. One of our favourite activities was to lie in the meadows and lace the pretty flowers into necklace and bracelets. We had our more active side too, when we would chase and hide, but generally we liked being close to nature.

Some days we would divert ourselves from our play and go to visit our dad in the forest on the days when he was working there. We kept out of his way of course because of the obvious dangers with saws and falling trees. I was fascinated by all of this, as was my sister, but she loved also to chat with the younger men working there. Sometimes when the weather was particularly hot, they would be stripped to the waste which made Sara giggle with excitement. They too loved the attention and would exchange pleasantries until my father noticed and shouted at them to get back to work.

The boy's days were a bit different. They often headed for the river which wound its way through the village. They would race across the fields and go into the woods. If they weren't fishing or swimming, they would build massive swings on the branches of overhanging trees and use thick ropes that they had found somewhere on the farm land. Sometimes we would secretly steal up and spy on them as they swung across the river. Their games usually ended up with them falling or jumping into the river from the swing. I remember once we ended up all laughing at Hans who had inadvertently fallen into the river. When he got out, he found his legs covered with leeches and try as he may he just couldn't get the little creatures off him. Before he and Johann could take their revenge on us for laughing, we were off.

On one of these occasions we decided to go across the fields and into the forest to play. It meant crossing a few farmer's fields and saying hello to various animals on the way. We could see the village herdsman in the distance on the higher slopes managing the buffalo that on a daily basis were left to his care by the villagers. As was typical, Sara wasn't content in just stroking the nose of the horse or

105

giving it a handful of grass to eat. When we weren't looking, she had climbed up onto the fence at the side of the horse and jumped on. She was a skilful rider in her own right, as we had our own horse back home which used to pull our cart, taking the family produce to the local markets. It didn't matter to her that she had no saddle; bare-back was fine.

I chased after her shouting vigorously as she cantered off across the field doing her own version of a cowgirl, pretending to fire her gun as she had seen on the films at the Saturday flea pit in Tigur Mures. When she returned to meet us, we could hear the farmer shouting profanities at us in the distance, so she quickly dismounted and we all disappeared into the woods. We all knew that once again Sarah would earn us a telling off from our parents when we returned home as the farmer would know exactly who had taken the horse. Out of breath, we collapsed in a heap in the clearing that often was our starting point in the woods. Sarah was laughing out loud and Katherina had fallen in with her infectious giggling. I however, was furious at my rebellious sister and launched into her, saying how we would get into trouble when we got home and how we would be kept at home for a few days afterwards.

Chapter Two

1938 -1943

By the time Sara and I got to our early teenage years inevitably our approach to boys changed. Gone were the attempts to avoid the boys, or to just secretly view them from afar. However, Sara and I had a different approach. As I had said earlier, I had always admired Hans and although he probably wasn't as good looking as my brother Johann, he was strong and reliable and would never let anyone down. In all honesty this is probably what most of the girls were looking for. Not Sara though, no way. As she got older, she liked to play all the boys along but was most drawn to those who were a bit more adventurous. This usually meant the more questionable elements in the village, whereas I valued dependability and yearned for someone who would fall in love with me and look after me into the future. Sara was more into being swept off her feet by the latest dashing Romeo-type, rather than thinking of security for the future.

I remember things coming together for me one Saturday night when we were with friends at the local dance. These occasions in the village hall were shared between our village and neighbouring Hohndorf. We girls were dancing with each other and hoping upon hope that the lads would join in and ask us for a dance. As usual, they were propping up the makeshift bar, each with a bottle of beer in hand. Our village boys stood in a group together and the Hohndorf lads were in another part of the hall when one of them decided to have a go at my brother. Apparently, one youth had asked Johann if on his behalf he would ask me to go out with him. It was probably designed to start an argument, but in any case, my brother knew that I had a thing for Hans, and so I assumed he told him to get lost.

Suddenly, Johann was surrounded by half a dozen Hohndorfers, all looking for trouble. It didn't happen often, but very occasionally these events could spill over into a fight and it was usually about girls. Just as I thought this was about to get nasty, Hans stepped in and firmly said to the young man that he had asked me for the next dance and this is why Johann had refused him. It looked a bit dicey for a moment, but I think that because of Hans' tough reputation, the rival villagers decided to back off. Hans then came across to me and asked if I would like to dance. Well, all my dreams had come true at that moment.

We didn't do anything directly after this for a while, although we both made it clear that we liked each other a lot. Sara got a bit impatient with this and worked on her own plan to push me into being a little bolder. She got the opportunity when Fasching came around just before Lent. This is traditionally carnival time and on just one day, called Weiberfastnacht, the women who choose to, can be forward with the men of their choice. The men who are chosen have to comply, but in return they are rewarded for their compliance with a kiss. I wasn't normally up to being bold in this way like some of the other girls and women in the village at this time of the year. However, as usual I had given in to Sara's incessant goading and challenged Hans in the street, by asking him to remove his hat. I placed it firmly on my head and then placed a big kiss on his lips, blushing as I did it, and then I walked off with his hat. I chickened out after a few steps away and turned, thinking the plan would have backfired, but to my utter relief Hans was grinning from ear to ear and clearly happy with my intervention.

After this we never looked back and we became an inseparable pair. Thinking about it now, we were made for each other. Both of us were the quiet, thoughtful types, and because of Hans' close friendship with Johann we had come to know each other well. For the next couple of years or so we would meet up in our spare time and take long walks into the forest. I used to confide in Sara as the relationship grew. I told her how, during one of these occasions, Hans had as usual politely asked to kiss me and that I had shyly agreed. Later I told her how surprised I was when suddenly he had asked if I would be prepared to marry him. I told her how I had nearly fallen over backwards and that I had finally agreed after I had got over the surprise. Two days later he plucked up the courage to ask our Dad, who gave his blessing to the proposal. We immediately started to plan the wedding for some time in the future.

Relationships were a bit different for Sara. She hadn't been planning for a romantic future and she continued to happily string along a host of boys. Over time I noticed that she had taken a shine to a lad called Martin Schmidt. He was a bit wild, which suited Sara, but he had a bit more personality than some of the other rowdy boys in the village. He was old for his age, if you see what I mean. He was accepted in their company by boys of an age above him and always seemed to know what they had been up to. I think Sara fancied him because he used to play her at her own game, pretending not to be interested in her. I think in this way he set her a different challenge and invited her attentions. Unfortunately, just as our relationships were beginning to develop our world was soon to be changed forever. To the outside world the war had started in 1939 and had been waging fiercely on several battlefronts. We were largely oblivious to this and had ploughed on living our life in the normal way. However, in August 1943, very suddenly the war arrived in Maldorf in very dramatic fashion.

SARA

Chapter Three

1943 -1948

1943 proved to be a momentous year both for myself and my sisters as the war dramatically entered our lives. This year was supposed to be so picture-perfect for me and my sister. It was to be the year when we were both to get married and start a new life with our chosen partners. In reality the war crashed unannounced into our lives and turned all our plans upside down.

We had been brought up in a protective environment by parents who themselves were purely focused on the family and life as small-time farmers. What was happening in the wider world hadn't registered in our household, but looking back there had been some signs in the years previous. It is no excuse, but I in particular had led a very selfish life, living happily from day to day without a care in the world. My family indulged my flights of fancy and I got away with some audacious actions because of my outgoing personality.

I had an older cousin Rosina who took an interest in the running of the village by being on the locally elected council. I didn't have much contact with her really, but knew she was the leader also of the Women's Committee and got involved with village matters. She visited our house occasionally and socialised with my parents, but they themselves were not political animals and within the family there were no discussions about what was happening in the wider world. Rosina had been critical in earlier years at the interference from outside in the workings of the local council. This had come to a head with the imposition on the village of a controlling group called the Volksgruppe who increasingly made decisions which affected community life. Looking back, we should have recognised this as an indication that the National Socialists in Germany were beginning to take an interest in the colonies, so to speak. At the time though we had no perception of the politics of Germany and its impact on the world.

 It occurs to me now that I should have read more into a funny incident that I heard Rosina tell my parents during a visit one evening. It had occurred towards the end of 1940 and the story became a source of fun in the village. A new priest had been appointed in 1936 and he quickly became unpopular as he couldn't keep his disdain for the community from his parishioners. Attendance in church dwindled and he was generally seen as a figure of derision. Before he came the church had been very supportive of the local community and very popular through its good works. Rosina was telling my parents that he had immediately aligned himself to the National Socialists in Germany and didn't consult the village council. It was so rare to hear any reference to politics in the house but we got diverted by what was ultimately a very funny story. It transpired that the priest had been given a vehicle by the German authorities to go about his duties and he was soon viewed with suspicion wherever he went. Rosina went on to tell my parents that the council had reported him to the church authorities about what she and her colleagues saw as his too close an allegiance to the German government. She said that this was strictly forbidden as the church was supposed to be neutral. They had made the point that instead of ministering to his parishioners he seemed to see his role as feeding information back to the German administration.

This is where the story took an hilarious turn because apparently when the information got out about the car his days were numbered. One afternoon, whilst he was giving his service in church to his ever-decreasing congregation, some older youths took the law into their own hands, stole his car keys and drove the car into the local stream. Looking back, I should have taken more from these events than just the funny story involved. These were probably indicators that we should have picked up about which way the world was going, but in truth the significance at the time was lost on us. Anyway, it was the final straw for the priest and he absconded, never to be seen again.

During the early part of 1943 both Sophie and I saw our personal relationships with our respective partners' blossom. She and Hans continued to meet regularly and began to plan for a December wedding date. I had finally given in and decided to concentrate my efforts on Martin, who had played hard to get initially. He had diverted me from my teasing of the other boys in the village and I became besotted by him. We would meet on the edge of the woods and take a drink and cigarettes with us. It became our secret that we tried to keep from the others. There was no planning for the future like Sophie and Hans and over time it was the buzz of being secretive and the physical excitement that we generated for each other that kept things going. Unfortunately, the inevitable happened. We hadn't been taking any precautions and I became pregnant. I hid the signs for as long as I could before confiding in Sophie. She was her usual understanding and supportive self and gave me the courage to decide to keep the child. I expected Martin to hit the roof when I told him, and true enough he was not happy at first. However, there were strong prejudices at work in our community and I knew that when our parents found out, there would be overwhelming pressures to get married. Which is exactly what happened on the 30th May that year.

Initially we went to live with his parents who had a house near to the church in the centre of the village. His mother was very unfriendly towards me from the start and made my life a misery. To put it mildly she was a real bitch towards me and it made me determined for us to have a place of our own. Our child Hildegarde was born on the 11th August but she was a sickly child who was subsequently to have a succession of illnesses. I continued to have loving feelings for Martin after the marriage despite the ongoing aggravation from his mother. However, I increasingly felt that his love for me was being tested once we were married and even more when Hildegarde was born. I don't know what it was but I felt uneasy and unsure of what might lie ahead.

Chapter Four

21st August 1943

None of us saw it coming but it is as chilling to me now as it was then. Just as I had given birth to Hildegarde and Sophie was looking forward to shortly marrying Hans, the war intervened with devastating effect. By now Martin and I had found a small place of our own near to the church. I personally had had enough of our stay with his mother.

My life had changed quite dramatically with the birth of our child and there was no more gadding about for me. I got lots of support from my mum who came round as often as she could to help out. Hildegarde was a very sickly child and needed a lot of attention above and beyond the normal issues with a young child. A succession of minor illnesses and visits from the community nurses kept me on my toes as well as the other domestic chores that went with having our own place. Martin wasn't much use around the house and he took off most days to meet with his mates locally. I had sensed a change in him once Hildegarde had been born. It seemed to put a weight on him that hadn't been there before. I had noticed that his attitude towards me had shifted once he had found out about my pregnancy, but this was worse. He just didn't seem to want to engage with the baby and showed very little interest in me once that sex was off the menu. His attitude was so different to Hans, and it made me feel somewhat jealous of my sister. This in turn made me feel guilty as she continued to do all she could to support me with the baby.

On one particular day I remember Martin returning mid-morning to the house and I could see something was up.

When I asked him what was the matter, he snapped at me:

- I've only been called up, that's all. I bumped into Johann in the village and he had just stormed out of his parent's house. He had received a letter saying that he was being called up to the war. I went straight around to my mum's and true enough I had received the same letter. I'm still trying to take it in, but Johann was fuming and saying he was not going to fight some stupid war.

On hearing this I was in a state of shock and I spat out:

- Oh my God. They can't take you. I need you to help me with the baby so they can just forget it. They'll have to drag you away over my dead body. Anyway, surely Hans will be able to stay as he is getting married soon.

Martin's foul mood continued and he shouted loudly at me:

- Of course, he'll have to go just the same. The letter specifically says that everyone of a certain age is to be drafted into the German army. That means me, Johann and Hans as well as all the other poor buggers in the village.

At this point he shot out of the house again and I burst

into tears. I decided to go to see Sophie to see what she thought of it all. Maybe our parents could find a way to avoid all of this? Maybe our cousin Rosina could use what little influence she had left in the village? When I got to their house Sophie was in floods of tears. I had rarely seen my sister so distressed as she was the strong one amongst us. I immediately went across to her and gave her a big hug before I let out a string of expletives at the top of my voice.

My parents were shocked at all this high-pitched emotion and my Dad tried to calm things down. I screamed out:

- What's happening Dad? Why are we involved in the war? I thought we liked the British and their gentle way of life. Everything sounds so civilised when we listen to the BBC Empire news channel on the radio.

My Dad tried to stay calm:

- I don't know love how we've got to this stage. The first I had heard of anything like this was in the village square last week when a couple of the old lags were speculating that the Fuhrer desperately needed support to fight the Allies. I was surprised to hear this at the time because no-one talks about politics. Football yes, but not bloody politics.

- It's not fair Dad. How are Sophie and I expected to manage without our men? What's the purpose of it all? Can't you get them to change the orders?

118

This time a bit more exasperated, he replied:

- Sorry Sara, and I wish I had paid more attention to what was going on in Europe so I could understand it more, but one thing I do know is that if the boys have been called up there is no going back, and that's the end of it.

Johann had been quiet throughout all of this before he chipped in:

- I'm more shocked than angry. Just as everything was getting sorted. I'm also feeling annoyed that we've all been sitting back and not paying any attention to the world beyond Maldorf. We've all had it a bit too easy and not seen what has been happening outside our little world. I'm going to have a word with Rosina, but I doubt she'll be able to do anything about it.

After a while I returned home and sat down to talk it through with Martin. By now he had calmed down and I presume he had had a similar discussion with his parents. In fact, when I saw him, he didn't look too perturbed. I had expected him to still be angry but he seemed to have taken it in his stride. He didn't say as much but looking back perhaps I began to realise for the first time that the war had given him the chance to escape from his new responsibilities as a father.

Two days later we all gathered in the centre of the village

to see our young men depart. They were heading for Elizabethstadt on the back of trucks, and from there they would be sent on for training by rail and then on to the war zone. There were tears in abundance and much sadness everywhere. The boys of course tried to put on a brave face, but we knew that they were very scared at having to go away to fight. We didn't realise it at the time but the war was by now well into its later stages by the time our young men were conscripted. It didn't take long after they left for us to realise that it was not just those who had been called to fight who suffered. We women left behind now had to cope with all their household duties and keep the smallholder tasks going, as well as dealing with the worries about our brothers and loved ones.

Chapter Five

1943-1945

As the months passed, we were itching for information back from those who had left for the war. The one saving grace was the occasional news that came back via the village priest's messaging system that he had set up with the authorities. Very early on, for example, we learned that Hans had been granted special leave to return from his military training for his wedding with Sophie, which had been planned for the middle of December 1943. I think that this was to a degree largely thanks to the priest arguing his case. It was possible only because Hans and his troop were still in training near to Munich and hadn't yet been called forward to fight on the frontline. That brought a degree of fleeting happiness back to our two families, and for a very brief period some joy into the wider community. Quite irrationally, as time went on, periodically these events re-kindled a strange sense of jealousy for me towards my sister, which I hated to feel at the time as it was totally unjustified. Just as I felt Martin slipping away from me it remained clear that, despite the war and their separation, she and Hans were totally at one with each other.

Time seemed to pass so slowly and life continued to be very tough for us. By now the Volksgruppe were in full control. At the same time as they were extracting resources from the community for the Reich, they also saw it as an opportunity to feather their own nests. They knew that the church services were well attended at that time. The new priest Karl Ungar had proved to be a pillar of our small society and the church itself was back to being the bedrock of our existence. The Volksgruppe officials insisted that the takings from the collection had to be split between the church and their group, supposedly to cover their costs. We knew this was going into their own pockets but were powerless to challenge it. In the past the priest would just have to go to the bishop to stop this but now things had been turned upside down. We could do absolutely nothing. All of this left us physically and emotionally drained.

On a personal level, things got a whole lot worse for me because Martin's mother did all she could to make me feel guilty about Hildegarde's illnesses. As if they were my fault. Of course, we had never got on with each other and this seemed like a good opportunity for her to continue her dislike of me. From my sister's perspective, Han's return home for his wedding had obviously been productive, as she announced a few weeks later that she was pregnant. It was good to see Sophie so happy at her news. However, as she got bigger with her pregnancy, she began to feel more anxious as time went on. I did my best to share my own experience with her, but of course having had such a sickly child didn't make for me being a very confident teacher. Also, none of our immediate friends had experience of motherhood and so she had to fall back on the re-assurances of our mother.

There were also the usual old wives' tales floating around, designed to help, but in general having the opposite effect.

- Be careful not to do this, don't forget to do that.
- Don't look at an ugly animal or your baby will resemble it.

Once the baby arrived it was different for Sophie. When Freddie was born, he weighed in at a healthy nine pounds in contrast with my poor Hildegarde who had been just five pounds. She still had the worry about Hans being away and whether he would return, but holding her new-born child and learning how to cope with his everyday needs was ultimately heartening and fulfilling to her. As time went on Freddie flourished but by contrast Hildegarde continued with her repeating illnesses. Some months later Hildegarde was rushed to hospital with dysentery and we were warned that she might not survive. Very sadly she was unable to pull through and she died shortly after being admitted. After this, Sophie did her best not to be too effusive about her young Freddie. I tried to reassure her that she mustn't let Hildegard's situation drown her happiness, but it did put a large black cloud over the family for a period. It was very sad when we all assembled to lay Hildegarde to rest in the cemetery on the hill beyond the church, alongside the graves of other family members. To try to keep my spirits up I kept telling myself that the war would soon be over, Martin would return and we would have children in the future.

Through all of this the priest did his best to supply us with information from the war. As well as his contact line he had established a local newsletter. Through this system we found out that our brothers were prisoners in separate camps in England. When bad news came back, he set up memorial services to those who had fallen during the war. We sang hymns and one of them in particular struck home to me. One line in it always brought tears to my eyes:

'Lying in foreign soil, so far from home, a small, quiet dome, shaped by the hands of friends.'

It made me so sad to think of an unknown soldier buried on the battlefield, his family unaware of his fate.

As the weeks and the months progressed, we continued to receive sporadic news via these means about the progress of the war. There were also occasional visits from German leaders from the front line to neighbouring villages, trying to drum up support. From the neighbouring village of Braller, which had been the former ministry of our priest, he told us that he had heard that one woman had invited people to her house to hear an important radio broadcast by Field Marshall Goering. When there had been no takers, she had berated her fellow villagers for not supporting the cause. The experience there supported the general view of scepticism that was felt in our village and probably others in the vicinity towards the German cause. It strengthened everyone's affinity to Siebenburgen rather than the so-called homeland.

As time went on there was little to cheer us but when a letter came back to us from Johann, via the priests messaging system, there was a brief respite. The letter told us a bit about the prisoner of war camp in England. He also talked a little bit about Yorkshire, the place where he was based. He described the landscape, the rolling hills and the woodland that surrounded his camp. I particularly remember it because on this occasion the priest came into our house very excitedly waving the letter. My Dad read it out to us:

"Hello mum and everyone. I told you in my first letter that I had been posted to a camp in the north of England, whilst Hans had been sent even further north to a place called Cumbria. I don't know what it's like in Cumbria, but outside the camp here there is some very beautiful countryside which reminds me of Maldorf.

After the initial shock of living in the camp with thirty or so other prisoners, life is a bit better than anticipated. I was surprised that we are allowed outside to work for a local farmer. We have a guard who stands on the edge of the fields watching us, but the farmer is a really nice man. He sets us tasks working in the fields, picking potatoes and looking after his animals. I guess he has come to trust us after the last few weeks working for him, and his wife too has been very kind to us.

Sometimes now we get to eat our lunch in the large farmhouse kitchen, where his wife prepares the most delicious cheese and pickle sandwiches. It's not the sausage and sauerkraut that we are used to, but is really tasty after a few hours working in the fields. She has promised to prepare something which she calls Yorkshire puddings.

I'm not sure what it is, but they see it as something of a local delicacy. Maybe I'll get the recipe and send it to you!

I've reached the end of my allotted words now, but will keep writing, and please make sure you don't worry too much about Hans and myself. I'm sure we'll be fine.

Love,

Johann"

The letter seemed to inspire the priest. Right at the beginning of his priesthood he had introduced the village to his hobby of breeding pigs. He had reared two breeds; the German Pure Pig and the Yorkshire White. Now suddenly the mention of Yorkshire encouraged him to organise a festival for the village. Everyone was invited to bring food and drink on the day, and my god did they come with their goodies. They laid out food and drink on long trestle tables and there was music from the local brass band and folk dancing. He had found the perfect way to raise everyone's spirits and the whole village joined in.

What we all found amusing was that as expected the villagers brought the usual food to eat – sauerkraut, wurst, sausages and Knodels – but the priest's wife had gone to the trouble of finding out about Yorkshire puddings and cooked some for the fair. We thought that we were going to get a dessert or something sweet, but it turned out that they were in fact savoury, not a pudding as we knew it, and served with a very rich onion gravy! Basically, it was just a batter like we used to make the spatzle, but put into bun tins to rise up. And my word did they rise up magnificently! We had no idea where she got this information from, to be able to produce the puddings, but it added to the excitement of the day. We all thought what a funny lot they must be in Yorkshire.

As the war progressed, we began to get little insights into how things were going. In the summer of 1944 at a Youth Festival set up for a number of villages, a German General came to tell everyone how well the war was progressing and he spoke of the inevitable 'Final Victory' for the Third Reich. We were all a bit sceptical about this as we had heard rumours that the Russian army had advanced to the Rumanian borders. I think that it was shortly after this that the Rumanian Government collapsed and the country swapped sides. News of this had been passed on to us by the priest following a visit he had had from an agitated community leader on the 24th August 1944. This person had heard on the radio about the collapse of the Rumanian government led at the time by Antonescu. We didn't realise then just how catastrophic this would be for the remaining Saxons in Maldorf once the war was over.

SOPHIE

Chapter Six

January 1945

I was really beginning to miss Hans and worrying that he wouldn't see Freddie growing up. We knew from the priest that the war wasn't going well for Germany and had heard reports of Russian troops on the border, but before the official end of the conflict, on the 9th January 1945, the war again walked straight into our village and directly into our lives. A day or two before rumours had been spreading like wildfire through the village that we had hoped were untrue. We knew something was up when we were confronted that fateful morning by the sight of Russian troops around the perimeter of the village. Their uniform was new to us, not like the Rumanian version that Johann and Hans had worn when they did their Rumanian national service. Neither was it like the German uniforms that had been around when they were being conscripted. We went to check out the noticeboard outside the church. Once there, our worst fears were realised as we read the sign;

All men and women aged between 15 and 50 years of age are hereby summoned to attend the village hall on the 11th January at 10 am, to receive news of their posting to assist the Russian war re-construction

Alongside the note was information about the items that each individual would need to have with them for the journey: food, blankets, clothing and shoes.

I immediately ran home and began to plead with my parents but I knew there was nothing they could do. I went round to see Sara to check that she had received the news and the two of us just sat and cried our hearts out.

In panic, a couple of our friends tried to leave the village, but they were unable to go anywhere as the village was already surrounded by armed police, Romanian volunteers and Russian soldiers. We had no-one to turn to as our village leaders had been dismissed, leaving behind just the Romanian bureaucracy to cover their backs. It appeared that anyone of German descent now had pariah status and worse was to come.

Two days later we all went to the village hall to check if we were on the list. Our worst fears materialised and there we saw our names printed clearly in black and white. Sara and I, plus our best friend Katherina, were all named on the first sheet with others of our age and told to assemble the next day. Maria's name was on a second sheet alongside those of an older age group, and they were told to report a day later. I didn't realise at the time that this older group were eventually taken to a camp in Siberia whilst we were destined to go elsewhere.

One dreadful irony was that a footnote at the bottom of the note stated that women with a child under twelve months of age were exempt. Just my luck, I thought, as by now Freddie was just twenty days over this deadline. My mother immediately went off and pleaded with the authorities on my behalf but to no avail.

Next day around thirty of us were herded into a long line and then forced to march the twelve kilometres to the assembly points in Elizabethstadt. We were a bedraggled sight as we waited to meet our destiny. It didn't help our nerves when a very frightening incident occurred where a young pregnant girl, who had been forced to march from her nearby village, suddenly started to give birth in the hall. All hell broke out as the guards pushed forward some of the older women from the villages to deal with this problem. They had accompanied us to the town to give comfort and support before we were taken away. In desperation the helpers cried out for blankets and boiling water as the young woman screamed out in pain, brought on by the physical effort of the birth and the horrors of what was happening to her. She and the child were whisked away and we never found out whether either she or her child survived. She didn't accompany us on the forthcoming journey, so we desperately hoped that she had been able to remain with her child.

At the time I was confused as to why all this was happening. It was only later that I found out that Russia had gained control of Rumania after the war and so this was presumably why we ended up in Ukraine. With hindsight it was clear from their actions that the Russians saw anyone of German descent as the enemy and fair game for exploitation. I also later learned from my parents that worse was to come for those who stayed at home. All assets, including land and property, had to be handed over to the Russian authorities and as things developed these acquisitions were transferred to local Romanian families. Some families managed to flee into Hungary, but those who stayed had the option to stay on as tenants in their own homes, whilst paying rent for the privilege. Some families were condemned to living in just a small part of their former home alongside their new "landlords".

We spent a couple of days in the holding camp because there were so many details to sort out. Some had rushed away from home so quickly that they hadn't got together the things they needed for the journey. A few young women had their young children with them and this meant that arrangements had to be made with their family back in the villages. Over these two days there was a constant to-ing and fro-ing back to the villages. In the case of people from Maldorf and Hohndorf, we were lucky that the priest once again took time out to help those who needed it. This, despite the fact that his daughter Helga was one of those forced to leave with us. Once the confusion was sorted, we were herded like cattle into rail trucks, heading for who knows where.

Chapter Seven

January 1945 – April 1947

As the train started to slow down, I suddenly saw the sign heralding our arrival in hell. There, in bold letters, a sign:

Camp 1004, Tschiasovar, Raion Stalino, Ukraine

The journey had taken over two days and proved to be a total nightmare. We were at least forty people to each truck, which had no seating. The toilet facilities had been grossly inadequate and consisted of a bucket in each corner of the truck with water and disinfectant. After just a few hours the stench emanating from the group was appalling. On top of the crowded situation, the heat throughout was horrendous and one unfortunate girl didn't make it. I could see early on that she was struggling and comforted her as much as I could, but I was also conscious of Sara getting increasingly wound up and so spent most of my time trying to calm her down. This had started earlier when we were being taken to the trucks. Sara was spitting feathers and cursing the guards, so I had to whisper quietly to try to shut her up. We also had Katherina in our carriage who was pretty shaky so I asked Sara for her part to try to help look after her. When we were leaving the carriage the poorly girl was too weak to move and although I felt terrible about it, we had to leave her behind uncared for on the floor.

The sight was quite chilling as we arrived at the camp and we were all petrified of what lay ahead. As we climbed down from the trucks everyone was shaking with fear following the horrendous journey. We hadn't eaten for the duration of our travels.

Once on the ground we were initially segregated by our gender and then taken in groups to the rough huts which lay within the confines of the camp. All around were high fences with barbed wire across the top and lookout towers at each corner of the camp. Outside the perimeter of the camp, I noticed a small graveyard with crude crosses laid out in random fashion. This sent a chill through my whole body. The huts were to be our living quarters for the duration of our stay, however long that was going to be. Inside, the accommodation was very basic, with small iron-framed beds, each with one sheet and a rough blanket. Luckily, my sister and I had stayed close together as we came out of the truck and we were not separated as we were moved into the dormitories. We also managed to get Katherina to stay nearby, and somehow, we managed to stay together as a threesome. I told my sister not to let on that we were related to each other as this might be used to punish us in the future by splitting us up.

Almost as soon as we sat on the beds, the guards barked instructions at us and told us to move outside and stand in line. We were all then given a primitive set of overalls, and a crude set of cutlery together with a book of vouchers which contained our daily food rations which we were warned not to lose. We were instructed that we must report at a set time, twice a day, to get our food in exchange for the vouchers. Later we were to find out to our disgust that the food was practically inedible. It consisted of a large bowl of unsweetened coarse porridge, served at seven in the morning, made largely from poor quality oats and water. The first time I tasted it was utterly awful, but as my hunger grew throughout the stay it came to be something eventually to be tolerated and then finally to be craved. Our only other meal was at seven in the evening as we returned from work. Here we received a small piece of stale bread and a bowl of gruel. This disgusting stew, was made up mainly of poor- quality root vegetables and very thin stock.

We were unlucky to have drawn a very bad-tempered person called Maruschka as one of the chief guards for our hut. She was quite charmless and seemed to take great delight in making life as difficult as possible. In the early stages the prisoners who had been there for a while quickly tried to take advantage of newcomers. Any opportunity to steal our bread or our belongings would be taken. We soon learnt the art of survival in camp and how to hide any surplus food and any personal articles of value. In fact, we quickly came to realise that bread was going to be the most vital commodity in the camp. This portable and palpable item had to be protected against theft at all cost, and served as a sort of currency. My sister and I developed the habit of saving a small piece of our bread ration each day in case we missed out on food for any reason. We had to find ingenious ways to hide the bread within the dormitory or on our person, as it was a key target for thieves. This reliance on bread became something of an obsession for all of us. Sara quickly learnt to use her well-honed negotiating skills to her best advantage with some of the male guards and her flirtations meant the difference eventually between getting a reasonable job, say in the laundry or kitchens, rather than the awful quarries or lime-pits.

Strangely, in some ways the work and the harsh environment were a useful distraction for me because at least for a period I could try to forget the pain I felt when I was on my own, constantly worrying about Hans and young Freddie. I tried not to show this in front of Sara because I knew she had different worries about Martin and whether they would get back together if we survived this ordeal. When I eventually lay down to try to sleep at the end of the day, that was the worst time for me, because all I could think about was my immediate family and how they were faring.

Unfortunately, Katherina was as bad at protecting her rations as we were good. Despite our continuous remonstrations to her, she struggled to keep her rations safe and could be easily duped. We did our best to help her and she was lucky for the most part because she had this protection. Sara and I looked out for each other and for Katherina. Early on, before she had realised how best to survive, Katherina had stupidly handed over her daily bread ration to one of the hard nuts.

- Let me hold that while you go to the toilet. Don't

worry it will be safe with me. You can't trust everyone in here.

Of course, this was the last that Katherina saw of that, but it taught us all a vital lesson. The other lever these veteran prisoners had, was the threat of violence to get you to hand something over. This was never likely to work in our small group as we had unity, but we also had our secret weapon, Sara. Initially the other prisoners were unaware of how fierce she could be and how strong and determined she was. The boys in Maldorf had learnt not to cross her and it didn't take long for the camp bullies to realise they were on to a loser taking on Sara and our group. In effect she became our special armour.

We struggled along, month after month, but life was hell. Without each other's support we might have fallen by the wayside, like some in the camp who didn't survive the hard labour and meagre rations. I suppose like everyone else we might have just soldiered on and hoped for the best, but a sudden tragedy befell us which was to lead us to hatch a plan to escape the hell-hole that was the camp.

As I have said, Sara and I had come to terms with the horrors of the camp. We learnt to cope with the constant craving for food and had devised crazy ways for either saving our bread rations or hiding it from our starving companions. Also, we were physically strong enough to meet the hard challenges that the work demanded. By contrast, Katherina was less equipped to cope with life in the camp and her vulnerability finally did for her. One day she came to me crying, saying she had lost her book of food vouchers. I pleaded with the guards to let her have a replacement but they refused. Even Sara's usual persuasive charms didn't work with them. For a while after this we each saved scraps of bread for her to try to make up for her loss, but we couldn't spare much because we also had to survive. Gradually she became weaker and weaker, and each morning it was harder to rouse her. I suppose she had been physically deteriorating over a period of time, but we hadn't really noticed how close she had got to finally fading away. The horrors of the eve of her death still haunt me. That night she had been too weary to engage in the usual pre-sleep banter, but even then, she had managed a faint smile and she squeezed my hand lightly before she lay down to sleep.

Chapter Eight

Next morning when I got up, I went across to her as usual to wake her but this time she did not respond at all to my quiet words of encouragement. I tugged at her shoulder to get a reaction but nothing came back. I saw that her eyes were fixed and cold and her pale body limp and lifeless. It took a while to sink in but when faced with her death I was horrified. I quickly roused Sara and with difficulty the two of us managed to dress her. The last thing we wanted was for her to be dragged out of bed by the guards and carted off for burial in just her flimsy nightie. We realised that unless we acted quickly this could have been the last act of decency and dignity that would be shown to her. We had witnessed earlier how callously dead bodies had been removed in the past, with the lazy guards getting a couple of the prisoners to help take away the corpse. I remember feeling terribly guilty, as if Sara and I had suddenly let down our friend. Of course, this wasn't really the case, because both of us had tried our very best for her in this brutal environment, but that didn't take away the feelings.

Then out of the blue, Sara came up with a crazy plan. She suggested that we volunteer to help bury our dead friend, as this would give us the means of getting outside the perimeter of the camp. Over time she had found a way to be very persuasive with the male guards. It didn't always work as we had found out with regard to the food vouchers, but this time she must have used up all of her charms as they agreed to let us help them bury Katherina. Sara had told me previously that one of them, called Helmut, had fallen for her charms and had previously confided in her that his sister had died in recent months. So I guess he was primed to be helpful. We asked for a little privacy and time to prepare her body for burial and used this opportunity to put extra clothes on ourselves which we might need later in the escape. We had hatched an escape plan some time ago, but had never fathomed out how we would get outside the camp. Here now was our chance, but without Sara's daring-do I would not have been able to go through with it.

By the time we had got Katherina's body out of the camp and into the graveyard the weather had started to get very cold. Winter was approaching and this part of Ukraine was particularly prone to early frosts. The ground was exceptionally hard as we started to dig and the two shovels we had been given were poorly designed for the job. We had carried her carefully to a plot at the far edge of the site, just a few hundred metres away from the cover of the forest. The guards took great pleasure in watching us struggle and shouted mock orders for us to dig faster. We just ignored them and said a quiet prayer for Katherina, whose spirit we felt was there with us.

We were probably at this for a couple of hours, by which time the guards were getting bored and less attentive. They kept sneaking off to have a crafty cigarette. Eventually we dug deep enough to bury the body and gently lifted her into the hole. She had lost so much weight in the preceding weeks that she was surprisingly light to move. Before starting to replace the soil, I had said to Sophie that we should time the last few shovels-full to coincide with one of the guards' cigarette breaks. This would give us time to complete the grave and make a run for it. When the moment came, we placed some wild flowers on the shallow grave that we had picked on the way. Then Sara signalled to me and we just took off, sprinting towards the forest. I thought we were bound to be stopped, but miraculously we made it to cover.

After about an hour or so of hiding we could hear the distant sound of dogs and the faint voices of guards shouting. We moved on a bit further, but we needed to finally settle and hide near to where the incoming wagons came in on the outskirts of the camp. During our stay in the camp up to that point, we had taken note of the location during a brief spell working in the adjacent quarry. It had always been in our imagination when planning our escape, that one day we would leave from here, using the outgoing trains to get away. The river was nearby and therefore I knew that it would be a good place to hide until there was a chance to escape eventually on one of the wagons, once it had dropped off the incoming loads of new prisoners and goods. We eventually had made it to the river bank and Sara told me to lie down and stay silent. By now the noises of chasing guards and dogs had receded and our task was to just sit out the darkness.

- Be patient Sophie. We need to lie low and wait for the light, then take our chance in the morning.

In our plan we had reasoned that the guards would be duty-bound to try to find us but that they wouldn't spend too much time on it because in reality we were expendable. After almost two years of hard labour in the camp we were a shadow of ourselves physically. The guards knew that new blood arrived on a regular basis, so we hoped that they wouldn't really give a shit about us and would move back to the camp after a perfunctory search.

As dawn was about to break, a dark drizzle enveloped the river valley. I remember squinting through the weak mist that shrouded the forest and feeling my senses dulled. For a few seconds my mind drifted and I was back by the side of the river in Maldorf. I could see the boys swinging across the stream and I could see my friends plaiting daisies. I thought about when I had married Hans and how we had immediately planned to have a family. I remembered how cruel it felt to be thwarted just as we had learnt the news that we were to have a child. It was all that we had ever wanted and I wondered where Hans was now and what was happening to my lovely son. Did little Freddie miss me and cry at night?

Then suddenly reality kicked in. It must have been five in the morning by now as I could hear the birds singing. I had been roused by the rumble of trucks which heralded the arrival of a train in the sidings, about two hundred yards away. From our cover we watched the guards first get the hapless prisoners to unload the new goods and provisions for the camp until they dropped with exhaustion. Then we saw them being unceremoniously kicked into line and taken back under guard to the camp. At this point Sara grabbed my arm and placed a finger on my mouth, urging me to stay silent. She pointed to the rear carriage of the goods train and signalled for me to follow her. The guards had moved forward as the train was about to push off and we had a few moments to make it to the carriage, slide back the door and hastily jump into the dark space. Unfortunately, just as I was getting into the carriage, I caught my arm on a jagged nail that was sticking out of the carriage door and I let out an almighty scream. One of the guards looked round, spotted us, and then of course the game was up.

Once they got us back into the camp we were immediately separated and put into the isolation cells that they saved for anyone who was deemed to have seriously offended. The first thing I felt was remorse that all our earlier machinations to get ourselves favourable treatment and softer jobs was now out the window. Once inside the cells the guards took pleasure in physically and verbally abusing us. I am so disgusted by their behaviours that even now I cannot bring myself to think about it and just want to block it out. We were given very meagre rations and a minimum of water. After a few days we were hauled separately before the camp commandant and told that we would be condemned to a future working in the quarries and lime pits. This was effectively an early death warrant as only the very strongest survived the work there for any length of time. We had spent the occasional day working there in the early stages of our imprisonment until we had made it onto lighter duties through Sara's good work with the guards.

 Our hours were even longer now at work and we had to eat separately when we eventually got back to the camp. In the dormitories we were ostracised by the other prisoners who had clearly been warned about communicating with us. I did at least get to see Sara each day as we were most times working together. However, we would be beaten if we attempted to speak with each other. Whilst I was toiling away, I couldn't help thinking about the contrast between what we were experiencing in this camp, and the different aspects of camp life that Johann had described in his first letters home. He said that he had to work hard and felt pretty isolated, but he was being treated with decency and allowed to retain a sense of individuality. Now suddenly I was left with a feeling of hopelessness, with all the spirit knocked out of me. I wondered how on earth could I survive in the future? I was gradually getting weaker and weaker with the harder work now forced on me in the lime pits. Something had to give or I wasn't going to survive.

SARA

Chapter Nine

April 1947 – September 1948

Since our re-capture and return to the camp we had lost all our previously earned privileges and condemned to a life in the most arduous work settings. Being younger than Sophie I was in a little better physical state than she, but in reality, neither of us could have carried on much longer. We had seen countless prisoners give way in the past to the constant pressures of the quarries and pits. Then, when all hope seemed lost, our adversity gave way to hope in the unlikeliest of ways.

It was early April 1947. Sophie and I were working together side by side in the quarry on this particular day. It was a dangerous place under normal circumstances as large chunks of rock were being blasted from the cliff, man-handled and then transported in metal trucks down rail tracks to be loaded onto lorries at the bottom. There, prisoners laboured all day smashing the boulders into more usable sizes before loading onto the lorries. On this occasion I was walking alongside the track above where Sophie was working when one of the rail buggies careered out of control, became de-railed and struck her from behind. It happened so quickly that she had no time to react to the warning shouts and she was knocked off her feet and pinned to the ground. She immediately passed out with the pain and shock that she must have been experiencing. Eventually, when she came to, she was surrounded by guards with me screaming at them to let me through. I could see that it was just her right leg that was trapped under the enormous weight of the truck. When she took a look at the damage to her leg and all the blood that was around, she passed out again.

I went with them as they took her to the sick bay in the camp. She woke up later screaming in agony and it was clear to everyone that she was going to need more skilled medical attention. I was beside myself at her plight and shouted at the doctors to give her more pain killers. She passed out again and I took the opportunity to ask to speak to the camp Commandant. I thought it would be a battle to get him to demand that Sophie get more professional help, but strangely he was very helpful and had already been in touch with the hospital in Kiev to arrange for her to be transferred for emergency surgery. I pleaded with him to let me stay with her through her treatment there and once again was pleasantly surprised that he agreed to this. I think he must have reasoned that it was better that I went with my sister rather than him having to free up a member of staff.

We were in the hospital for nearly seven days. The staff there let me stay in the bed next to Sophie and provided me with food which I could prepare for the two of us whilst she received treatment. She needed a couple of operations on her badly smashed leg but her condition improved to the degree that the hospital decided that she could return to the camp. Nevertheless, she was still in a bad way and in constant pain. When we got back to the camp, we were called in to see the Commandant and I had prepared another speech to try to convince him that Sophie be given light duties. I was fearful for her future and worried about how she would possibly survive back in the camp. Luckily, the camp commandant must have worked this out and realised that if she stayed, she would be a passenger and a drain on his resources. To my utter surprise he told us that we were both going to be sent to a new camp towards the west where Sophie could recuperate further and eventually be put to work in a less physical environment. The commandant must have cursed us initially because of the injury but I think the situation he found himself had to be dealt with within the framework of the Geneva Convention as effectively Sophie had become a victim of the war. Unwittingly, her serious injury had proved to be a bit of a saviour for the two of us.

Two days later we were discharged without any idea of our destination. We knew that we were being sent to a place where we would still be held captive and have to work, but in a more suitable environment for Sara. When the time came, we put our few things together and then we were shoved onto a truck. By now Sophie was emaciated and very weak and still very dependent on me.

Chapter Ten

September 1948 – Moschendorf Camp

We started on this new venture by being transported yet again in one of the awful train wagons that had originally brought us to the first camp. Conditions were less cramped and the sanitary arrangements slightly better as this time we were sharing the basic facilities with just half a dozen or so others. They weren't as ill as Sophie, but all had struggled in the camp and needed some form of rest or treatment. It was a long journey as we had to have an overnight stop at a place called Frankfurt an der Oder. From there we were taken by lorry towards Erfurt and then on to a town called Hof, which was near to the German border. A few miles further on, and still on the Russian side we began to see the signs of the new camp to which we had been transferred. The whole site was very large with a number of dispersed buildings sprawling over several acres.

As we drew close, I noticed a large forbidding sign which read "Moschendorf Konzentrationslager". This filled me with dread and my anxiety level went up a few more notches at the sight of high barbed wire fences and sentry towers. Thankfully our truck passed by the main gates of the camp and went on further to the front of what looked like an old hospital building, outside the perimeter of the secure camp. Many years later I checked up on the details of this place and confirmed the awful history associated with it. For a period, it had had a very dreadful history.

Thankfully, after the war had ended, the dreadful atrocities committed inside had ceased and it was now being used primarily as a hospital and rehabilitation centre.

The work in this second camp was infinitely better than in Ukraine. It felt more like a rehabilitation centre as a lot of the prisoners were recovering from either injuries or illness as a result of the heavy work regimes they had experienced in other camps. I was feeling pretty strong, but Sophie was very much still trying to re-gather her strength. We both found ourselves allocated to working in the gardens, tending the fruit trees and vegetable patches which fed the camp. For this we were reasonably well fed and life was just about tolerable, but when we returned to the camp there was the same disrespect from most of the guards. I suppose we should have been thankful at least that Sophie's ongoing frailty had played a part in our being given relatively light duties.

Security was also more relaxed and there was no protective perimeter fencing, just the large grounds and gardens surrounding the buildings. It was however very remote and I guess this was thought to be its best defence to keep the prisoners from leaving. Around the camp there were dense forests and beyond that very steep mountains. For the short period that we were there I continued to receive treatment for my damaged leg and over time my mobility improved.

To a certain extent I was happy that Sophie had the time

to recover some of her physical strength in the new camp. It gave us both time also to reflect on what had happened to us over the past couple of years. True, I was homesick and still worried about my family and whether Martin and I would make a go of it together in the future if we survived. I felt hemmed in here and right from the beginning determined to try to escape. I told myself it would be easier here because the security was less tight. Sophie though, was more resigned to a lengthy stay there, and continued to fret and worry about Hans and Freddie. My free spirit still lived on inside of me and I quickly felt penned in again. I tried to convince Sophie that when she was sufficiently strong, we could try another escape, but she was very reluctant to contemplate this. She told me to go on my own if the camp got too much for me, but there was no way I would leave her behind.

I couldn't get the thoughts of leaving out of my mind. Everything here told me that the chances were good. Sophie's accident, hospitalisation and then removal to this camp had by chance brought us close to Germany. If we could escape at least it was believable to think that the journey from here across the border into the west was possible. Our work in the camp was much lighter than previously as we had been allocated work in the gardens. I could see that Sophie was building up her strength day by day and that she would eventually have the strength to make it if we got out. The biggest thing in our favour was that security here was much lighter. There were still loads of guards around and we were being watched closely as we worked, but there were no high fences anywhere.

The other thing that struck me was the opportunities that might present themselves because of the fairly relaxed way we were allowed to socialise with each other after our work and evening meal. After dinner we were allowed some leisure time which was usually taken outside by the campfire. I thought that we just needed to be patient and wait for the right opportunity to come along. Plus, I still needed to get Sophie on board. It took me some time, but eventually I wore her down and laid out my plan. The May Day celebrations were imminent and the camp authorities were planning a big celebration. I had calculated that there would be good deal of alcohol involved and that the guards would be complacent during the celebrations. I then laid out my detailed plan to Sophie, who somewhat reluctantly agreed.

Then the day finally came and the May Day celebrations began. As I had reckoned, the guards largely left us all to ourselves that evening and were more intent on having a good time. The more alcohol they consumed the less vigilant they became but we had still to be wary as there may be prisoners on the lookout who had been planted to check on proceedings. We chose our spot near the campfire, as close to the forest as possible and waited for the appropriate moment. In planning for the escape, we had put together some essentials which we had secreted under our clothing. We wore an extra layer of clothing and hid the small amounts of money and food which we had been able to squirrel away, including our precious bread. Fewer guards were on duty than normal and they were drinking heavily. They seemed more bothered about toasting their hero Stalin than caring about what we were doing. In truth it was very tense on the night trying to choose the right moment to make a move, and we hesitated on a number of occasions. Sometimes we would be about to go when a guard would suddenly return from a cigarette break. On other occasions the attention of one of the inmates seemed drawn to us just as we were about to leave. Then I took my chance, and when the guards were nowhere to be seen and everything seemed right, I whispered to Sophie:

- Now Sophie. This is it. Follow me and don't look back.

Despite her doubts she obviously trusted my survival instincts and took my lead as we fled into the forest. We probably both thought that we would be pulled back before we got very far, but we managed to get to the cover of the woods without being noticed and hurried as best we could as darkness fell. We seemed to have been walking for hours until we felt sure that we weren't being followed. Progress was slow because Sophie was still very limited with her bad leg. That night we slept out in the open, pulling some leaves and branches over us for cover. At no time did we pick up any hint that we were being pursued. Unlike the time of our failed escape, there were no dogs to be heard and no voices from chasing guards. Next morning, we walked for some time and took a lengthy break as we could see a hilly area in front of us. We climbed for what seemed an eternity and ate the last of our food as we reached the top.

Looking down into the valley I pointed out a rail track and some signs of habitation.

- Come on Sophie. Look, we've made it. Let's get down there.

I shouted this so confidently to her, without really knowing what lay ahead of us next. This encouragement seemed to work because going downhill Sophie seemed to have a bit more of a spring in her step. When we got to the bottom, I had a sense of deja-vu as once again it seemed that our escape was going to be dependent on rail trucks. Perhaps we would have better luck this time. When we arrived by the track there was no one about and so we stole onto a freight wagon and prayed that it would eventually take us in the right direction, wherever that was. We lay low for quite some time and took the opportunity to rest. Suddenly there was a bump as the train took off. A couple of hours later the carriage stopped abruptly and I looked out to see where we were.

The voices of workmen rang out in the near distance. By now daylight was breaking through and I could just make out the name of the station where the train had stopped. It read "Coburg", and I wondered where on earth we could be. I realised that we couldn't afford to stick around as the voices were getting nearer and I was determined that we would not be caught again. There was a strong smell of steam and oil and the noise of railway engines in the distance. In the past all of our previous experiences of wagons and train journeys had been negative, and at this moment I was filled with dread. I just had to leave.

- Wake up. Get your things. We need to get out of here quickly.

Quickly we gathered our few belongings and carefully pulled open the sliding doors of the wagon. We made our way along the line in the opposite direction to the voices. Within a kilometre or so we hit some fields, and in the distance saw some lights, just as dawn broke.

- Let's get some cover and lay low for a bit.

Sophie followed obediently as we entered some outbuildings to what was clearly a farm with cattle in the adjacent fields. In the corner of the barn, I could see a pile of what looked like turnips, presumably the feed for the cows. By now we were starving. We had learnt to cope with minimal food whilst in the labour camp, but it must have been two days since our emergency rations had run out. Foul though it was, we bit into the raw turnip, devouring it as if it was one of the luscious pears that we used to grow in Maldorf. It was clear that we couldn't stay here for long as the farm workers would be up and about soon, but we had got some brief relief, before we edged gingerly out of the barn and slid carefully away from the farm.

We found ourselves on a small country lane and the signs at a crossroads pointed the way to various places. Taking pot luck and trusting my sense of direction, we chose to head west towards Bayreuth. At this stage we had no idea where we had got to on our journey. I suspected that we were still on the wrong side of the border, but hopefully well on our way to Germany.

We seemed to have been walking for miles, when a farm truck pulled up and the driver offered us a lift into town. The driver must have felt sorry for us as he dropped us off at a local cafe and bought us a coffee. He asked what our plans were, but not in a suspicious way. I think he was just curious at seeing two slightly dishevelled women looking for a lift in this quiet rural setting. I shifted the conversation a little in case he wanted to find out more of how we had come to be there. He told us that he had always lived in the village and that his parents owned a farm locally. He was a single bloke and obviously happy to have something like this distract him for a while. We obviously hit it off because as he took off, he left a ten roubles banknote on the table.

After the farmer had gone, the cafe owner came over, presumably curious to know what we were about. I was still very wary about our position and although we were by now well out of reach of any search that they might have started, I was not sure where we were exactly. I decided to use the note to buy a couple of cakes, which seemed a bit obtuse given the nature of our last meal, but this might give us a foothold with the cafe owner, who I hoped would tell us where actually we were.

After a bit of small talk, it transpired that we had found our way to a place some eighty kilometres north of Nuremburg. Not bad I thought, drawing on my limited grasp of geography. I did know that Nuremburg was in Germany, and definitely in the right direction for Munich, and therefore that this was a good place from which to strike for South Germany. The cafe owner proved very kind to us and he could see we were in a bit of a state. While he was chatting to Sophie, I had a quick check of my armpit as we hadn't had a proper wash or shower for days. He was a bit diplomatic about this and said that he was travelling towards Nuremburg the next day and offered us a lift. He also said that we could take a shower upstairs if we wished. He shouted up the stairs to his wife who came down to see what the fuss was about. She was also surprisingly kind to us and re-assured us that they could be trusted.

She led us up the stairs and whilst we took it in turns to shower, she laid out some food for us and some old clothes of hers. Over some tea we later found the confidence to explain to her what we were doing and why we were there. She in turn told us that she had heard dreadful stories about what had happened after the war and said we could stay the night if we wished. She warned us that we would have to decide how to negotiate the border between the two countries, as there were fences, minefields and check-

155

points everywhere.

Following a comfortable night our trust was repaid, and true to his word, the café owner took us part of the way towards Nuremberg. He told us that the borders were just a few kilometres ahead and that there were land mines in certain areas to defend the crossing points. Having been dropped off a distance from the border we proceeded cautiously. I could see a checkpoint ahead in the distance. I pointed towards a forested area and ushered Sophie to follow. As we cleared the forest there was a tall wire fence stopping access through the border, but no immediate sentry points were in evidence. At the other side of the fence there were signs warning that land-mines were in place. This didn't deter me after all we had been through. I spotted a small tear in the wire fencing by one of the posts, and was able to pull on the fence to create a small gap for us to crawl through. We took our life in our hands, assuming that the mines were still live, and put our trust in God to see us through. I guess we were just lucky to get through unscathed. Maybe we deserved a break for all we had been through.

After another hike of about three hours we arrived in Hof, quite close to Nuremburg. We knew to head for the Red Cross offices in the town centre. After a few stops to ask for directions we found their office and they were very helpful. The staff member organised a night's stay for us in a hostel. Having gone through their extensive records they located the whereabouts of Hans, and then made arrangements for us to be temporarily accommodated in a village called Stettenhofen further south and nearer to Gersthofen where he lived. We were told to wait here and after an overnight stay we were advised that we would be picked up later by Hans' brother Georg. The farmer and his wife were very kind to us and they prepared our first real meal for such a long time. I still remember every spoonful of the dumplings and roast pork they made for us. Just twenty-four hours later the farmer drove us to the station at nearby Langweid where Georg was waiting for us. After much hugging, and the usual tears, we took the next train to Gersthofen.

SOPHIE

Chapter Eleven

September 1949, South Germany

I remember arriving with Sara at Augsburg railway station and feeling that I was so lucky to have made it to Germany. When I saw Hans in the distance walking along the platform, I was overwhelmed to have found him again after all those years. I ran across the platform and flung myself into his arms. He picked me up effortlessly and we kissed passionately as if we were making up for lost time. I hadn't forgotten about Freddie, but for now my heart raced at being back with Hans. We took a train just two stops on the line towards Munich. It was all new to me so when we got off at Gersthofen I had no idea what to expect.

I was still on cloud nine as Hans took me to the house that he was renting in Mozart Strasse. It was a ground floor maisonette with a shared garden. Once we had arrived, he told me that he and a friend were planning to build their own property further down the village, but they had only just acquired the land. I told him that I didn't mind that we were in a rented house as I was just so pleased to be with him. Being still very weak from life in the camps and from the horrendous trek after the escape, I took some time just resting and trying to get my strength back. I was itching to get into the garden to help out, but hadn't the energy to do so. Eventually time, and the patience of Hans, got me through. I also took great comfort from the occasional visits of Sara. She had found accommodation in a flat nearer the centre of the village and had found a job in a local factory.

As time moved on, and life got back to some form of normality, I spent most of my time in the garden, tending the flowers and beginning to grow tomatoes and vegetables. Hans began to spend more time away, building our new home with the help of other ex-Maldorf families. I became friends with some of the wives, and they introduced me to a wider circle of people in the village. Gradually, I became stronger, but I had to take some care as my dodgy leg still gave me a lot of pain. What amazed me was the amazing access I had as a newcomer to medical services and the kindness shown to me by the Doctor and nurses at the surgery.

Although our life was good, we constantly fretted about Freddie who was still in Rumania with his grandparents. We wrote to him and received letters back but it wouldn't be until February 1958 that we would be able to welcome him into Germany. We had learnt from letters from our parents that Freddie was very close to his grandfather and as he grew older, he used to work alongside him and they were inseparable. It must have been a terrible wrench for my father when Freddie eventually was given permission to join us in Germany. This eventually happened because of the persistence of our relatives in Rumania, with the help of the local priest there. Once he had joined us, he told us how he and his best friend in Maldorf, Horst Zikeli, had

had to walk several miles to Elizabethstadt to get the necessary documents from the French embassy who were dealing with such matters at the time as there was no German embassy. Freddie could remember the exact date that they got their papers. It was on the nineteenth of September 1957. At the end of January 1958, the news came through to us that the children were free to be re-united with their families in Germany. A few weeks later, both he and his best friend Horst finally made it home.

You can imagine the utter joy that we felt as his parents to receive him into the family fold. He had been just two years old when I had been taken away to the camp and he had never seen his father before. As a consequence of Freddie being brought up for so long by my parents, and because he was so close to his Grandfather it took him some time to form a close bond with his father. However, once he had settled, he was a very easy boy to care for. He was very fastidious at school and completed his education, but like his father he was very much into practical skills. Hans helped him find work with a local builder as soon as he could leave school at the age of sixteen, and he took to his trade exceptionally well.

This would prove to be really useful when a couple of years later Hans decided to build our own new house in the nearby village of Gablingen. We had got on very well sharing a house with the Zikelis in Gersthofen, but Hans was very driven to save money and build our own detached house in the country. Gablingen was just a few kilometres away, and was a small hamlet consisting of a few traditional farms surrounded by open fields and forests. Freddie and Hans carefully chose the plot on which the house was to be built and sourced the timbers for the house locally. Between them they had the necessary skills to complete all of the build, with occasional help from the other ex-Rumanian friends we had come to know locally.

One thing was clear; people from Siebenburgen did all they could to support each other in their new environment. Freddie eventually moved out and found a place of his own, but in the mean-time he had formed a close bond with my sister Sara who had been going through some difficult times. Sometimes her choice of partners had been poor and unfortunately, as a result of this she fell out of favour with Hans. I was stuck in the middle of this and tried to placate all parties, but Freddie became very close with Sara and visited her as often as he could, much to Hans' disapproval. It didn't stop me and Sara still caring about each other, but it created a bit of tension within the family which made for difficulties in the future.

By the time we were able to buy the land and start the build, our second child Horst had been born. Horst was a bright and thoughtful child, very popular with his schoolfriends, and not a moments trouble at home. As Fred moved out to start his own family Horst became a great help to Hans and myself in the home. Soon after he married Adelheid after a short courtship. She had recently joined her family from Hohndorf in Rumania.

Chapter Twelve

Autumn 1992 – Gablingen

My life with Hans since my return from the camp many years ago has generally been a period of happiness and quiet. Very little that you could call remarkable happened to us, and given what we both went through during and after the war, that is to be thanked. Occasionally our happy life was punctuated with sad times mainly concerning family bereavements such as the premature deaths of my brother Johann and his wife Flo. Thankfully, I have some very happy memories to fall back on when Johann, and his own family from England came to visit us in Germany. It was such a joyful event to see him arrive with his wife Flo, and their young son Johnny. Johann had his own wartime stories to tell, and went through with us his experiences in the prisoner of war camp in Yorkshire. His had been a somewhat different experience of captivity to my own, and unlike me he was happy to share it with others. By contrast, I couldn't bear to think of what had happened to myself and Sara, let alone speak of it to others.

Another tragic loss was that of my son Freddie to cancer. I have periods when I am immensely saddened by these tragic events and would not have been able to bear the sadness without the support of Hans, Horst and Adelheid. There were other issues to wrestle with over the years which tested the family, but I guess this is what happens in all families.

I am thankful that I managed to keep my close relationship with Sara despite the friction that built up between her and Hans over the years. From Hans' point of view, he got very frustrated by what he saw as her disastrous relationships with different men. From her point of view, he was interfering in her life and not allowing her to make her own choices. It blew up big time over a decision for one of her children to be adopted shortly after the birth of the child to another man who had chosen to desert her after the birth. I did my best to support her and try to allow her to make the best decision she could for herself, but she was in a poor state of mind at the time. We were both extremely upset that she had been left alone to cope in this way and disappointed that once again she had fallen into yet another bad relationship. All of this reinforced the view in some quarters that she was promiscuous and irresponsible. As her sister, I knew better. I knew that she felt very unloved and insecure inside and that these poor relationships stemmed from this and her wanting to be loved. I tried unsuccessfully to be the go-between between her and Hans, who eventually took a very dispassionate view of her.

At least now I can think about the happy times when Johann had visited us with his young family. They had all so enjoyed the visits and he was looking forward to coming again a year later after his last trip here. He told us that he intended to work some extra shifts at the colliery to pay for it. All of this was suddenly taken away by the shock news we received from England. We were in shock when we received a telegram from Flo advising us that he had died in a freak mining accident. We were saddened at not being able to get to his funeral, but it was just impossible for us to attend. We sent a letter of condolence and some flowers, but had to suffer our great sense of loss at home.

Later in life Hans and I had visited Johnny and his family in England and were able to visit my brother's grave. It had taken us years to agree to visit our family in England. His son, Johnny, had regularly kept in touch and visited us here in Germany every other year. We had become very much home-birds, so the trip to England was our first and only venture by air. We enjoyed staying with Johnny and his wife Joy by the sea-side at Flamborough on the East coast of England. We could walk from the house with Sammy the Labrador and walk to the beach at South Landing, taking Jonathan and Anna, their children, with us. All of this was very different for us and an experience we would not have missed. Hans couldn't get over seeing the wide-open countryside of the Yorkshire Wolds, and the large fields of wheat and corn. He also appreciated being taken by car to see his brother in Carlisle and to recalling his own camp life near to there in Wigton. But we were so glad to get home to our comfortable and quiet life.

Looking back these happy events only compensated a little for my traumatic experiences during the war years and immediately beyond. The years in the camp and the privations I suffered with my sister, took a huge toll, both physically and mentally. It might have helped to be able to talk about these things but I kept them bottled up. Without Hans and my kind son Horsti and his lovely wife Adi, the rest of my days would have been unbearable. As it turned out, I have taken much solace from the good life that we have all been able to make for ourselves in Germany and the friends we have made with other families who managed to escape Rumania.

The sense of routine which had kept me going over the years was very different from the regime of survival that I had learnt in the camps. There it was a means to setting daily milestones to make sure that we got through the day in one piece and then repeating it time after time. Once I was back amongst my family members a more re-assuring and satisfying routine returned. This was more a throwback to my earlier life in Maldorf. Of course, there were new things to learn about life in Germany. Better opportunities to get good health care. More choice of things to buy in the shops. New activities to try out that just weren't available then. However, and this is true also for other ex-Maldorf people who came to Germany, our hearts still lay in the past in Siebenburgen, and we carried on much of the lifestyle we had valued before.

Although new opportunities were there, our old routines and habits returned. We were still drawn to the land and invested large periods of our daily time to the garden and to growing the fruit and vegetable as before. Our Saxon roots survived as we made friends with the other Maldorf families who had made it here like ourselves. Over time, every second year, families from Maldorf and Hohndorf came together to a different town in Bavaria for a weekend festival and we shared our memories and remembered the traditions that had served our ancestors so well over the centuries. At home I continued to serve the same food that my mother had prepared for us and that her mother had done for her. I learned other recipes alongside these, and of course as the decades unravelled newer food styles and trends emerged, usually through the requests of the children. I took this on but I continued to focus mainly on the old Siebenburgen recipes. The more traditional habits of preparing and preserving foods rooted us firmly with our past.

It could provide some amusing situations though. Our English visitors loved the different meals that I prepared. They were particularly keen that I serve them the traditional recipes. I guess it was good for them to have a change from the regular meals back home. I remember during one visit in October, Hans came back to the house and opened the boot of the car. As he began to unload, Johnny's eyes almost popped out on stalks as Hans took out a couple of dozen heads of cabbage and began to take them down into the basement.

- Vas ist das? Varum so viele?

I laughed at his stilted German, grabbed him by the hand and led him down into the cellar. I showed him the large barrels that I used for making sauerkraut and showed him all the different ingredients that I would be using later that day. After lunch, he and his girlfriend Joy were interested in joining me in the cellar to watch me start the process off. First, I put a large quantity of dill sticks, the herb savoury, horseradish roots, quince, chilli peppers, salt and water in the bottom of each barrel. Each head of cabbage had to have the hard stalk element removed and then I put salt in each of them, stalk side up. On top of this I put a board and then this was weighted down with a heavy stone or brick. I explained that each day for two months I would have to come down into the cellar and put a hose pipe in and blow air into the mixture. I explained that every so often I would refresh the water and add salt until after two months or so it would become acidic. At that point I put it into large jars to last the year and use it as a salad or in main dishes such as Szeged goulash. I was pleased that they took such an interest in this, and that Joy took the trouble to write down the process. I decided to use this as an opportunity to serve some of last year's supply with traditional sausages when we next sat down to eat.

As the subsequent months passed, I found myself getting more and more tired and my leg continued to pain me. I cursed on a daily basis the horrors of the camp but I kept this to myself. What kept me going was the love and support of my family and being able to take myself back to those happy times as a young person in Maldorf. Ours had been a challenging life at times, but we had come through it all and made a good life for ourselves.

Epilogue – October 1992

Hans, Horst and Adi sit at the front of the church in Gablingen, with Sara and her four grown up children in the row behind. Behind them are two hundred people who have assembled to say farewell to Sophie. The minister reads from the brief history that Horst has put together for him, laying out Sophie's amazing life for the congregation to take in. Those who are there who did not know Sophie closely are amazed to hear of the events that she endured through the war years and beyond.

The minister speaks reverently about her and about her quiet, caring presence in the village, where she has been well known and respected. Many of the congregation have come from different parts of Bavaria as they are part of the dispersed Saxon community who once lived in the Siebenbergen area of modern-day Rumania.

Traditional hymns are sung by those gathered, accompanied by a choir made up of elderly singers, all from Sophie's original village of Maldorf. The tears flow as Hans is clearly moved as he sits on the front row, next to his son and daughter-in-law.

Very poignantly, the audience sing from the hymn "Ich bin ein gast auf Erden",

I am a guest on earth: here I no longer roam

Rather, Heaven receive me, that is my one true home

I am travelling to the grave, in the hope to find

God's eternal blessing, and my final peace of mind

Hans removes the tears from his eyes and is comforted by his son. The next hymn is 'So nimm den meine Hande' and the guests sing with passion:

O take my hand Dear Father

I cannot walk alone

You lead me to my blessed end

I sit beneath your throne

At the end of the service the congregation files out in turn and follow the family group out into the street and then in double-file down to the nearby cemetery. At the head of the procession is a family friend, holding a large cross, and she leads the party through the cemetery gate and down towards the empty grave that has been prepared in advance. As they pass through the gates, a brass band strikes out a traditional Saxon tune, welcoming the cortege to its destination.

The crowd gather by the grave, with a large marble headstone sharing Sophie's details, all beautifully engraved. Next to her plot, a space for Hans has been reserved for the future. In keeping with tradition, the mourners approach the grave in turn and throw earth and then a solitary rose onto the coffin. From here the group retires to the local village hall to celebrate the life of their loved one.

SARA

Chapter Thirteen

September 1948 – August 1951

After my sister's funeral I find myself continually going back to those early days in Germany, after our horrendous experiences in the labour camps. Our lives have taken very different paths but we remained close as sisters despite some real ups and downs between me and Hans. I brought a lot of what was to happen to me on myself, but when I arrived in south Germany I was feeling very much alone. Sophie had her Hans to share a new life with. I had no one close living with me and very much needed someone to love and to hold. Martin hadn't returned after the war but I knew he had survived and decided to stay in England. I assumed that like Johann he had found someone else, but the difference was that my brother had no ties back home, unlike Martin. He had deserted me and this pained me deeply.

When we arrived in Germany after our escape and long trek from the border, we were met on the platform at Augsburg station by Hans and he explained that he had arranged for me to stay initially with himself and Sophie until I could find an apartment of my own. Ok, so initially I had them around me, and they were kind to me, but I felt that I was getting in their way. A bit illogical, because they were perfectly friendly as you would expect, but I wanted to find a life of my own. That same old urge again not to be cooped up and pinned down.

So, it was strange at first trying to settle into my new environment. Despite the unerring assistance of Sophie and Hans in the early days, I needed to have a life of my own. I would go out each day, just to stop myself from going crazy. I would walk around the village and the local park. The place I loved the most was to walk along the banks of the river Lech. What a magnificent sight it was and to think that its source was so far away in the mountains. I learned this from a stranger I met in the local allotments that ran seemingly for miles in parallel to the river. I was walking past and spotted him tending his vegetables and I took the trouble to say hello. I've never found this bit difficult. You know stopping to talk to complete strangers. Particularly men. I don't know why I have always felt comfortable in their company. Maybe it's because I was a bit of a tomboy when I was young. I would play with my sister and the other girls but was always envious of the rough and tumble of the boys. My way of engaging with them was to tease them and I found it easy to string them along.

Anyway, this man was probably in his sixties and very weather-beaten. He obviously spent much of his time outdoors and reminded me a lot of my Dad who always seemed to be out in the fields when I was young. This person was very kind and invited me to have a cup of tea as we sat outside his shed. Well, I call it a shed, but it was a very rough and ready construction that he had cobbled together from left over wood and old doors. We got talking and it was so good for me to be able to chat freely without any pressure. He showed me around his plot which was mainly vegetables with a few flowers thrown in. I told him a little bit about why I had suddenly landed in Gersthofen and he very kindly just listened and then said that I could drop in any time as he was usually at the allotment most days. And this is what I did. On my way down through the village I would stop at the various farms that were on my route and enquire about work but nothing transpired. It was my allotment friend who got me my first break. When I told him about my need to find a job, he told me he knew a local farmer and he said he would have a word with him. Some days later he told me that if I called at his friend's farm, he might be able to help me, but it was a few miles out of the village and I would have to make my way to Langweid where the farm was located.

 This was just the break I needed and I borrowed a bike from Hans and took off into the Bavarian unknown. Luckily the farmer was a nice man and he and his wife were most welcoming. He said that he would give me a try but he couldn't pay me much. What he could offer was pretty basic accommodation and food. They were very plain rooms, shared with another couple of refugees who were also employed to help on the farm. It wasn't grand but it gave me the space to try to start a new life for myself, make some new friends and have some independence. Being close to Gersthofen, I was able to keep in regular contact with Sophie

I hadn't heard from my husband Martin for some time and hadn't a clue as to what he had done once the war had ended. Imagine my shock when one day in February 1949 he suddenly showed up in the village without any warning and made contact. Once I had got over the surprise of seeing him, I had to get over a bigger bombshell when he told me that he had returned to ask my permission for a divorce. I couldn't believe this and it took some time for me to realise that what was happening was in fact true. He coldly told me that he had met a young girl whilst in the camp in England and they had settled in a small town on the east coast there called Scarborough. I didn't know what to do and so turned to Sophie for advice. She acted as an intermediary between us and helped me to weigh up the options. I wasn't thinking straight, so was grateful for her calming influence. It became clear that he wasn't going to change his mind, and after a short while he left for England, giving me a forwarding address. In the end I followed Sophie's advice and decided that I did not want the hassle of going through a contested legal battle at the time when I was trying to establish myself in Gersthofen. Reluctantly in the end I gave him my permission.

Chapter Fourteen

Late 1951 - 1954

I stayed working on the farm for just over two years. The farmer was called Josef Kaiser and he and his wife were incredibly kind to me. On my times off work, I had kept in touch with Sophie but of course she and Hans were building their new life together. In the past, approaching new people and making friends had never been a problem for me. Everyone knew me as the life and soul of the party, but the wartime experience had left me somehow scarred and fragile. I tried not to show it, but inside I felt afraid and unsure of what lay ahead. Looking back, as a result of this insecurity, I made some serious errors of judgement in my relationships, and found it difficult to commit long-term to anyone.

This was particularly true when I left the farm and took up a small apartment on the edge of Augsburg. I had managed to find some part-time work and in truth I met some dodgy characters there. Things went downhill when shortly afterwards I was admitted to hospital with severe pains in my abdomen. It ended with an emergency operation to resolve problems with my uterus, and then some time resting. I was advised by the doctors that the difficulties I was experiencing was likely to do with all the hard work that I had to endure in the labour camps.

Whilst in hospital I met a man who was a real charmer. He was called Adam and he was a refugee formerly from

Czechoslovakia. I realised too late that I was too free and easy with him and ended up in a sexual relationship which went badly wrong from my point of view. I got pregnant with my eldest child Rosalinde, and when he found out that I was carrying his child he duly took off without accepting any responsibility for this. What he hadn't told me was that he was also in a relationship at the same time with another girl, and I found out later that he was soon to marry her. Again, I had fallen into a trap of my own making, thinking again that I had met someone who loved me for who I was. Regrettably once more it proved that he just wanted me for sex.

This period was a total disaster for me because he immediately denied paternity and whilst this was being contested, he labelled me as a whore and someone not fit to have a child. As a consequence, the authorities decided that my baby Rosalinde should spend some time in a children's home in nearby Murnau, whilst the dispute was sorted out. It took me a whole twelve months fighting through the courts to get her back and to have him tested for paternity so that he could take some financial responsibility for his actions. Although she was too young to remember I never forgave myself for inflicting this on Rosalinde. I don't think that she bore any real grudges about this, but I always had a feeling of shame about what happened. Sadly, the lessons hadn't sunk in as I was about to let myself down further.

I continued working whilst Rosalinde was away and visited

as regularly as I could. She was only a baby but I reasoned that if I visited, and was allowed to hold her she would not lose the bond with me as her natural mother. When she was allowed back to me, I had persuaded the authorities that it would work because Sophie had agreed to provide child care during the days I was working. Thankfully by the end of this period with Sophie's support, I was successful in the courts as a result of Adam's blood test and finally it was decided that he would have to provide financial support until Rosalinde's eighteenth birthday.

By now I had a new job working in the laboratory service at the old military base, again at Stettenhofen. I was very unhappy within myself at this time, but used to get a lot of my frustration out by cycling the ten kilometres or so to work. These events, brought on my erratic behaviour, were beginning to drive a wedge between myself and Hans. I can see now how I was getting a reputation as being promiscuous, because again whilst working in the new job I became pregnant to another man. Whilst there I had met an English teacher called Johnny and I fell again for his charms.

Again, repeating the pattern, once he found out about the impending child, he left me. I couldn't see it at the time, and blamed others for my misfortune, but of course now in the cold light of day looking back on these destructive relationships I can see that they were the result of my feeling insecure and wanting to be loved. By the same token now I can understand to a degree why people wanted to label me as a bad woman. At the time although I hated it, and hit out at those who wanted to criticise me for my behaviour, I deep down felt that I deserved everything I got. The truth was that these bad relationships were sending me into a downward spiral, and for a period I felt totally out of control of my life. I gave birth to another child, this time a boy, who I never got time to bond with. Against my wishes I was pushed into the process of adoption and I have regretted this ever since.

I was in no fit state to resist at the time, and everyone was trying to do what they thought best I suppose. Hans had been in touch with the authorities and also the brother of my first husband had got involved. Hans and he had maintained a distant friendship and now they saw a perfect solution to what was in their eyes an embarrassing family situation. The couple involved had unfortunately been unable to have children of their own, so here was the fairy-tale answer and the authorities bought into it! Sophie gave me her support as best she could, but the men had their way and the adoption proceeded. This created a rift between Hans and myself, from which neither of us fully recovered. The only saving grace for me was that Sophie never lost faith in me and Freddie used to visit me regularly and remained a true friend, at the expense of some anger from his father.

It took a while for things to settle down after all this upheaval. I rented a flat close to the railway station in Gersthofen and found a new job with the Michalke company in Langweid-Foret. I worked on textile machines, making socks, tights and gloves. I could keep up my cycling as the factory was between Langweid and Gerstofhen. This was a good period for me as over breaks I would sit outside at lunchtime eating sandwiches and chatting with the other refugee workers. Unlike people before they weren't judgemental and I gradually got my self-respect back.

Ironically, it was my love of cycling that got me into my next relationship. I had been into the bicycle shop near the railway station, looking for some more comfortable cycling shoes. I had bought the new shoes and ridden off in them, without realising that I had left my walking shoes behind. I hadn't noticed anyone else whilst I was shopping, but apparently a man had been in the store at the same time. Shortly after I had left, the shop-keeper noticed my shoes and explained what had happened. Very kindly, the man had offered to drop them off to me later. The shop-owner knew me well and happily handed over my address to him. Imagine my surprise when this polite and kindly man turned up on my doorstep and presented me with the shoes. He introduced himself as Franz Kerle and after a cup of tea we agreed to meet a few days later for a coffee in the village and gradually we became friends.

Chapter Fifteen

1954 – 1978

My relationship with Franz flourished and we continued to see each other regularly and then finally he moved into my flat. He had a steady job and worked regular hours and it looked like finally things were working out for me. These were indeed happy times and it wasn't a great shock to either of us that I became pregnant. He had worked hard to persuade me to have a permanent relationship and I was cautious at first, given my track history with men. I had by this time anyway decided to settle with him so the pregnancy cemented things for us and I accepted his offer of marriage.

Our first child together, Hildegarde, entered the world on the twelfth of September 1959. We had a few good years building up the family, but disastrously events intervened once again later that same year when Franz was diagnosed with tuberculosis. I couldn't believe how cruel life could be. I was eight months pregnant and expecting our second child, Elisa. He had to have surgery and lost his job. He didn't handle being on benefits well and began to drink heavily.

Despite this, in the early days he remained a good father and for a period he cooked our meals and played with the children and settled for a while. Unfortunately, he became more depressed and the drinking became heavier and he spent less and less time in the house. I was desperate and needed to keep working for my own sanity but also to pay the bills. There were times as the children grew up when they had to fend for themselves and I wasn't there for them often when they needed me. In truth it must have been hell for them at times being left alone and seeing their father go downhill. My children were teased by the other children at school about their weird parents; the loose mother and the alcoholic Rucksackdeutsche of a father.

Although Franz's health continued to deteriorate, we were blessed with another child, Robert, born on the eighth of August 1968. Robert was a joy as a baby and as he grew older, he came to be something of a positive mascot for the family. To myself and the children Franz remained an enigma but he was basically a kind and thoughtful person. His dependency on drink I think had developed as a way to appease his failing health. He never stopped loving us, although at times it must have seemed the opposite to the children, being left alone while their father was out drinking and mother working. His health remained an issue for a further ten years or so until his death in February 1978.

As the children grew up our lives improved, once I found a better job nearer to home. I was lucky to find employment with Hoechst chemicals in Gersthofen. This was an internationally renowned company which paid its employees well. I had a great boss, Herr Frank, who took me under his wing and showed me that there are good men around who don't just want you for their ulterior motives.

He was kind and visited us at home, bringing small gifts for the children. In appreciation I cooked for him when he visited and we had from then on always enough food to eat and usually the best ingredients, as I loved to try my best with the meals that I prepared for the children. When I got down, as I often did, Elisa would grab hold of me, get me to sing and dance and talk of the happy times when I was a child in Maldorf. I saw a bit of myself in Elisa; always wanting to seem happy on the outside, but perhaps churning up with self-doubt on the inside.

Chapter Sixteen

Gersthofen – 2011

More recently my life passed fairly normally for me, in contrast to those difficult post-war days and then the various problems I had with my menfolk. Despite their slightly chaotic upbringing, my children have grown up to be responsible adults and have built a good life for themselves. I now have a couple of grandchildren and even two great grandchildren. Their visits give me a great amount of pleasure and when everyone has visited and left, I think back to the good times.

I remember a trip that Elisa and I took to Dinkelsbuhl to take part in the Siebenbergen festival that takes place in a different Bavarian town every second year. Here Transylvanian Saxons meet to share their experiences, reminisce on the past and live out their customs and traditions. Even the local German restaurants took the trouble over this weekend to showcase traditional meals. We were able to tuck into sour soups such as Ciorba de perisoare, which was served with traditional meatballs. Alongside we had Zacusca spread onto bread. I loved this mixture of tomatoes, peppers and aubergine. Also, we ate Mici which were beautiful meat rolls with dollops of mustard. After this we overdosed on the sweet delights on offer. I loved the traditional festival dish of Hanklich; a cake made from bread dough, flour, eggs, milk, butter and sugar. Over the two days we visited special displays which depicted the traditional Siebenburgen lifestyle. For all the visitors the experience reinforced the everlasting bond that the Transylvanian Saxons had with their past and which our family still clung on to.

There are also such happy memories of the times we had when my brother Johann visited Germany with his family before his tragic accident. He came a couple of times with his wife Flo and son Johnny. Later also, after he had passed away, it was so beautiful for me to welcome Johnny and his own wife and children. These fleeting trips have left me with happy thoughts about my special brother. Just recently I was able to meet up with Johnny and Joy and their daughter Anna, at a family get together organised by Elisa. Anna had also come with Jez her boyfriend who hailed from Sri Lanka and who got on so well with our older boys. It was so good to be able to give Johnny a big hug and to have our photograph taken, which I will cherish.

There is also so much to remember about the earlier visits from our English family. I remember shocking Joy a little on one occasion when she visited my flat with her children. I guess they must have been about three and five years old at the time. We were chatting and laughing and I offered the children an ice-cream. Their eyes lit up and off I went to fetch it from the freezer. What Joy wasn't expecting was the lovely sauce that I had laced on top of the ice-creams.

-   Try this lovely Tina Marina

I chuckled with pride as the children tucked in happily.

- Do you mean Tia Maria? Joy blurted out.

Then we all just laughed and Johnny said:

- It won't hurt just this once.

As my own children grew up, they used to love meeting up with Johnny on his visits with Flo and Johann. I remember them coming home so excited at meeting him at the outdoor swimming pool in Gersthofen. They had bought him a semmel with small fish inside and he had initially been unsure what to do with it. He clearly had never seen such a thing before but after trying it he couldn't stop talking about it and asked for another.

Chapter Seventeen

One thing that keeps coming back to me was just how lucky I was to get the chance to see my elder sister Maria again when she visited us in Germany. I think it was in 1973, but my memory is sometimes a bit hazy. We had been sent to different labour camps after the war and then she had returned to Rumania whilst Sophie and I set up our new lives in Germany. We had managed to contact each other by letter and Hans and Sophie had made a couple of journeys to Maldorf in the interim. On these trips they had taken medicines which they had found were unavailable in Rumania as she, like Sophie, had suffered badly because of her hard labours in the Siberian camp.

Hans and Sophie had managed somehow to get permission from the authorities to let her come on a brief visit to see her family and to get treatment in Germany. What was even luckier was that her visit coincided with one from Johnny and his wife Joy, from England. Johnny was so happy because he had never had the chance to meet her before. I remember how excited we had been waiting on the platform at Augsburg station to greet Maria. We hadn't seen her for the best part of twenty years. I tried to keep a positive face when I went to hug her, but I was so shocked at her physical appearance and condition. She had aged so badly and it was clear that she needed our help. Not that she complained, she was just so happy to greet us all. It was early evening and Hans had decided that we would get a quick meal in the city and so we went out to a local restaurant close by the station. It was getting dark and as we walked down one of the main shopping streets the street lights were just coming on.

As we walked through the city, I could not believe the look of wonderment in Maria's eyes. She was glancing randomly around the street and constantly repeating the word "Paradise". She told me later that she couldn't imagine so many bright lights and so many beautiful goods in the shop windows. Back home she told me they were used to many planned power cuts and there were few street lights in Tigor Mures, the nearest city. Also, in the cities and towns in Rumania, she explained that the shelves in the shops were empty of all but very basic goods.

During her stay she told us that after leaving the camp in Ukraine she had wanted to return to Rumania to look after our parents and for a time she also helped to look after Freddie. She told us that when she got back home to Maldorf, life was very different from the times we had before the war. For a short period, the family house and land had been seized by the Russians and handed over to local Rumanian families. They had had to rent back their house and pay money to these local people. Maria said that during these times it had become completely lawless and some of the Rumanian people had tried to seize more than what they had been officially granted. She told us that on one occasion our father had challenged someone who had tried to steal his threshing machine. He was so protective of his equipment and had been the first person in the

186

village years before to get a tractor. He had heard that someone was about to try to take his thresher and he and Fred had hidden it under straw and then tried to fight off the intruders. Our father had to run away from them and only saved his skin by hiding down the well in ice-cold water. Eventually, when it was safe, the Saxon villagers came and rescued him.

Maria was also full of stories about our father and he was definitely a character, just as I remembered him from my childhood. She told us another story about when he and Fred were out with the horse-drawn carriage, when some communists had attacked them. Apparently, a young man came to help them fight off the assailants and father used his horse whip to deter them.

She went on to tell us that after a period the house sequestrations were reversed, but the lands owned in the countryside by the family were taken over on a permanent basis by the state and became communes. This stressful period had a lasting effect on the families treated in this way and this was to manifest itself in a deep distrust of the state and of their native Rumanian neighbours. Her previous letters had described these poor circumstances she had found herself in after release. Rumania by then had become a hard-line communist state and people were forced to work on large farm communes or in state-owned factories. Wages were pathetically low and food and basic goods in very short supply. She told us that goods were incredibly expensive and that for example a bag of sugar cost the equivalent of one week's wages. The letters had described how her health had suffered badly in the camp and that once home in Rumania she struggled to keep up with the hard work that she had to endure just to make enough to live a very basic existence. All this was very apparent by the state of her health during the visit. She had married in recent years and spent much of her time caring for our elderly parents who still lived in Maldorf. As a condition of being allowed this short trip, the authorities had made it clear that she could only travel alone and her husband must stay behind. She knew that she had to return to Rumania or else her family would pay the price.

Her visit was only for a few days but this gave us time to get her seen by a doctor and to get some basic medicines for her. Her legs were badly ulcerated and again the nurses were able to bathe the wounds and put on some fresh dressings. Her condition reminded me very much of how Sophie had been in the aftermath of her injury in the camp. Even now, all these years on, Sophie's injured leg gave her trouble but now at least she was able to get ongoing health treatment. I knew that Maria would have no such luxury when she returned and so we had to get her as much help as we could in the time available. Perhaps the prospect of her getting the treatment paid for was a consideration for the communist leaders in letting her go for a few days. At least they would be relieved of the burden of dealing with her medical conditions.

The years in the camp had taken their toll on her physically as well as mentally. Even though the visit was short-lived, it was clear that Maria was getting much-needed relief for her ailments and she was very grateful. When we got back to Hans' house on the first evening of her stay, we were anxious to hear more about how things were back in Maldorf.

Of course, we had heard some of the troubles in Maldorf via letters, but it was good to get it first hand from Maria. She told us how everyone had been pressured to leave their farms and small holdings, and work in the state factories and communes. She said that there the work was very hard and the pay almost non-existent. There was an active black market for goods and a lot of underhand dealings. The state as a result had imposed an extra tax for stealing that they took directly from their wages; assuming therefore that everyone was untrustworthy. To proud people who had previously made a good living off the land this quickly became a disincentive to work for the state and many had reverted to relying on their small-holdings and their traditional crafts. Families were pulled closer together to share the little that they had. Together they grew crops, reared pigs and poultry and made their own garments. It was subsistence living but she said they would rather go short than work for the State.

There was a cost to this, she said, in that now they had to release a share of what they produced, to go to the local state-run markets where the proceeds went into the coffers of the local bureaucracy. She also told us about their once beautiful house, with its courtyard and big front gate. In the past so elegant, now it had fallen into disrepair and desperately needed attention. The deterioration started during the period when properties had been sequestered from the German community. The local Rumanians who had been given ownership of the properties had done nothing to maintain them and had hung on to the rental payments that had been forced on the Saxon families and had undertaken no maintenance on the houses. Although they now had their homes and land back, they couldn't afford the materials for repair or renovation which in any case were in short supply.

She told us of a recent visit they had made by horse and cart to Tigor Mures. They had wanted to see what was available to buy with their limited funds. When they got there the stores and shops were just shells in comparison with earlier days and they found nothing of use. Her story just kept getting worse. She said that the men had taken to smoking and drinking whatever was available to them. They had dug out their old stills and started again to make schnapps as before. Now though they had to use potato peelings and fallen fruit rather than the pristine grapes and plums that they used before. She said that the mixture of poor schnapps and cheap cigarettes had a peculiar ageing effect on the few who had returned after the war and also on the newer generation of youths. Before the war the men were strong and athletic. Now they were like old men before their time. They slouched around and stood on corners or under trees, bemoaning their lot to the next melancholic generation.

One good thing that she had to tell us was about the period when she got home from the camp, towards the end of the 1940s and re-joined our family in Maldorf. Although life was hard, she clearly had enjoyed helping our parents look after young Freddie. By then he was five years old and had grown into a strong young child. He was going to school and had many friends in the village. Clearly Freddie was not short of love and attention and they continued to pass on positive news when it arrived from Sophie and Hans. They were able to encourage him that eventually he would meet up with his parents in Germany and in this way kept him in touch as best they could with his parents.

What was clear to us from her stories and her appearance was that life twenty years on in Rumania hadn't improved. In fact, On the contrary it had got much worse. Very few of the menfolk had made it back from the war and the older women had literally been left holding the fort. She talked very disparagingly about the leader, Nicolau Ceausesco. She said that the Saxon people saw him as a Russian puppet leader and corruption had got much worse since his arrival. Nothing could be bought at face value. You had to know someone who knew the right person and the right place to get any scarce goods you needed. Luckily, the remnants of the farm still existed and the women had fallen back on basic skills to live what was a very stark subsistence life. The three days of Maria's stay went so quickly, and we wept buckets when we saw her off on her journey home on the platform at Augsburg station.

 Most of the time now I see my family but I am now too frail to go out with them on visits to the zoo or in the local cafes for a chat and a cake like we used to. I've had to move in with Hildegarde recently and she and Elisa have hired a hospital bed for me to be comfier. Hildegarde's daughter is a nurse and she comes to turn me regularly and to make sure I am ok. I am more or less confined to the indoors, but I have found that it has freed me up more to talk to my children about the past. Before I kept most of it to myself. Maybe one day somebody will write about my experiences and make a story out of them. Certainly, there is a lot to write about. Life is ok now and I have my memories to keep me going. I'm too old now for the buzz and razmatazz which I used to live for but I am content and eventually will leave this life with some pride.

Epilogue

October 2012 – Langweid – Bavaria

Six strong men carry the coffin into the crematorium and lay Sara down on firm wooden trestles. Then the priest takes the audience through a moving service, relating her life story from a peaceful childhood in Rumania, through the war and her eventual incarceration in a labour camp in Ukraine. Then a little about her better life in Bavaria.

The aging choir break out into song. All of them exiles from Maldorf or nearby, once again meeting to pay tribute to a well-loved friend. How many more times will they be able to meet to sing the traditional anthem from their beloved country. They sing not of Germany or of Rumania but of Siebenburgen.

-   Siebenburgen, Blessed Land
    Land of Plenty and of strength
    Protected by Carpathian Mountains
    Your seed grows into our green crops
    Land rich in gold and wine

More passionate verses follow, then the loud finale;

-   Siebenburgen, Our Sweet Homeland
    Our dearest Fatherland
    Let us greet thy wondrous beauty
    And around thy many sons,
    Place a strong uniting band

193

Before she is taken away her three daughters and her son stand silently. Elisa, lays a large plaited loaf on top of the coffin. The children pass between them the green harmonica that their mother carried around with her every day. Slowly the coffin trundles down the conveyor belt and is gone.

Later at the reception, one of Sara's visiting cousins from Nuremburg asks Elisa to explain the riddle of the loaf of bread and she tearfully repeats the story that her mother had felt only able to tell them just before she died. Throughout their childhood Sara's children had always been unclear as to why every day without fail their mother would place a piece of bread in her coat pocket when leaving the house.

In the end she had been able to relate to them how the fear of being without food in the camp had haunted her forever afterwards. In the camp she had seen a close friend, Katherina, die through a mixture of fatigue and starvation. She told the children, with a lump in her throat, how Katherina had lost her food stamps for the bread early during her stay and Sara and Sophie had been unable to give up enough of their rations to keep her alive.

Elisa sighs with relief, says to the aunt "Now thankfully, Mama can finally relax, taking her daily bread with her."

Part 3

Hans

Chapter One

January 2017 – Gablingen - 9.30 pm

I love sitting here on this balcony, looking across the fields to the forest. I can't believe that I've survived so long given what I've had to go through in the past. Just a few months to go and I'll be celebrating my 100th birthday. I know that my hearing is poor and I have had the occasional fall, but my mind still feels as bright as a button. I regret that it's been a while since I've been able to go out, but I can still do most things for myself.

I built this house with my eldest son Freddie over fifty years ago to accommodate all of my family. Sophie and I took up the ground floor accommodation, with Horsti, our youngest, having a bedroom alongside us. Freddie moved out shortly afterwards, got married and had a place of his own a few miles away in a nearby town. The house was on four floors, with a big basement and then accommodation on three levels. The top floor was a bit like a penthouse, with bathroom, kitchen and living quarters of its own. It was originally designed to be an apartment for Horst when he came of age, then to let out possibly, but once Horst got married, he and Adi moved into the second floor, which had all the facilities they could need. I decided eventually to hold on to the top apartment solely for guest use. I'm glad I did this because over the years we have had many family members from England come to stay with us. The basement occupies the full footprint of the building which provides space for storing food, housing the boiler and generator and has a large play space, which is mainly used for table tennis.

Freddie had several happy years with his own family and we kept in touch periodically, but sadly he died some time ago. I miss him so much, as I do my lovely wife Sophie, who also passed away a few years ago. I guess I cut a bit of a sorry figure sometimes now because of my sense of loss. On the positive side, Horsti and his wife Adelheid are a very happy couple and they continue to live on the second floor and provide me with exceptional care. Adelheid had come over as a child from Hohndorf, which was the neighbouring village to Maldorf where I had been brought up.

Now, I cling to as much of my independence as I can. I take most of my meals' downstairs on my own. All my food is prepared and brought to me by Adelheid and she and Horsti help me with a few personal chores. Each day they pop in several times to check that I'm ok and occasionally I choose to eat with them, but I know I am always welcome to join them at any time.

I'm very forgetful these days, particularly about more recent things. Ask me about events in the past and I can recall things from way-back. Because of this, I must be a pain to look after sometimes, but Adi and Horsti are so patient with me. I miss the daily walks I used to take in the adjacent woods and the chats I would have on the way with various neighbours and friends. I used to stop and chat for ages with my immediate neighbour, Doctor Muller. He would tell me about his children who had successful jobs in the city. Further on, I would talk with Frau Bender about the weather, and she would tell me how her cats were doing.

My only big regret is the way that my care has impinged on the life-style of Horst and Adi. They undertake their care of me with deep love and attention even though it is several years since they have been able to go on the skiing trips with friends to the Italian Dolomites or the Austrian Tyrol. Nowadays they unbegrudgingly give over their lives to ensure that I have the best of support.

It's getting late now and the low clouds outside have begun to envelop the forest. There is a slight mist which begins to hide the view across into the distant hills towards Munich. I had better start to think about bed-time.

Next morning

I'm in my element here, at the back of the house in the morning. Adi has kindly brought me a coffee and yesterday's newspaper. The local news is full of successful business and new development. Since I settled here after the war, a lot has also happened in the country at large. Germany has achieved a hard-won security which is a million miles away from the uncertainty in those immediate post-war years. When I came to Gablingen all those years ago to choose a plot for the house, this place consisted of open fields leading on to pine-forested woods, with the occasional old farmstead dotted in between. Back then I selected the plot because of its rural location. In those days from the building site there was a rough track next to it, on the edge of fields of corn and rows of turnips and then leading out onto the unspoiled forest. In those days I imagined that those fertile fields would remain farmland into the future and that I would be able to walk these paths with my growing family. True enough, although as the years have passed the small community has grown into a more bustling place, this end of the village has remained largely untouched and my family has flourished here.

One change for the better has been the development of a Riding School opposite. The children from the village and beyond visit and look over into the ménage with its steady stream of fine horses. It has become a constant source of joy to me, to be able to look out of the window and see the toing and froing of visitors to the stables and the day to day exercising of the horses. All in all, my life here has been good and satisfying. There have been periods in the past when things had been quite the reverse. I still think about those times but perhaps I'll save up the memories of bad times until another time.

Looking back, there were some funny moments. I used to breed rabbits in a little lean-to that I had built at the back of the double garage. They were for us to eat eventually, not there as pets, and I had my own system of little dials on each cage telling me when they were fit for slaughter.

Telling this now, it all sounds so gory, but we used to do this in Maldorf, and it just came naturally to me to want to continue. Plus, it was healthy food for the family. Horsti used to bring his school pals round to visit, and they were particularly engrossed by the rabbits, and would want to see them and stroke them out of the cages. In order to explain why some cages were now empty I would say that they had escaped and also make up stories about what the strange dials were for! I think the most bizarre explanation I gave was that it allowed us to know when their birthdays were.

Chapter Two

Maldorf – August 1943

As we were growing up as teenagers, my best friend Johann was more interested in girls and playing football, and wouldn't be drawn on politics. I had been a little bemused when, a few weeks earlier, we had learnt from our village leaders that all of our community had been granted full German citizenship from The Fuhrer. However, I hadn't made the connection that this could herald problems for us. I had tried to engage Johann in a discussion about what was happening in the wider world and just as he had been when we had done our earlier national service in the Rumanian army, he wouldn't be drawn.

- We'll be alright, Hans, the war is miles away from here. Our government has a happy knack of avoiding things.

Then, that fateful morning, I was so angry to hear from my parents that I had received a letter from the German government calling me to war. As usual they had opened the family post when it arrived earlier. Johann and I had been working in the fields as normal and I had called in to have lunch while he went off to his family to grab a break from work.

I learnt later, whilst we had been doing our training, that there had been a need for more soldiers to boost the war effort as Germany was struggling to hold off the Allies. Hitler had come up with the idea to give citizenship to the many exile German communities scattered around Europe and beyond as a device to boost numbers. He had devised his own name for theses scattered groups and labelled us all as "Volksdeutsch". We hadn't known who to believe prior to all this as to how the war had been going. The local Volksgruppe that had taken over affairs in the village just seemed to spread propaganda as to how well Hitler's campaigns were going. We got a different story when we listened in to the British Empire News on the radio. So who was telling the truth, we thought? None of it seemed real until that fateful letter dropped onto the mat. Rumania had a long history of following which ever way the wind blew and we didn't think that the country would play any significant part in affairs. How wrong we were.

The spell that Johann and I had earlier completed in the Rumanian land army had at least given me some idea about the rudiments of war, but this did not prepare me for the awful times that lay ahead. We remained friends despite our different views on what was happening in the outside world across Europe. As I said earlier, Johann tended to brush any thoughts of the conflict aside, wheras I had a more traditional pro-German outlook on life. I had been more prone to listen to the debates held in the village square when the old-timers started to relive the past. Some of them would go on about the impositions placed on the German state after the Great War. Others argued against the idea of fighting but I was drawn to some of the arguments which talked of a sense of loss of pride that Germany had had to endure. Johann stayed out of the arguments and was much more rooted in the Saxon way and driven by our more ancient traditions. I appreciated that too, so we were never at loggerheads over this, just that I knew not to engage him about current politics. Not that I knew what was going on really anyway.

Looking back, it is so strange how ill-prepared we were for the awful eventuality of the war. Maybe our Elders in the village had somehow decided to protect us all from the horrors of the outside world that had now had come to bite us. We had probably also underestimated the influence that the new Volksgruppe was having on us and how little control our own leaders had.

These new developments unleashed a tremendous sense of injustice in me as I had made plans to marry Johann's sister Sophie in a few weeks' time. This latest news came as a real bombshell to me, just as it must have felt to Johann. I was a couple of years older than him and therefore supposedly should have been a bit wiser, but it didn't quite work that way. For his part, when I caught up with him to discuss the news, Johann was fuming.

-   How fucking ironic is it that our little community can exist successfully here in Rumania for all those centuries, in splendid isolation from the so-called Motherland, without any hand-outs and then just when we are doing so well on our own, we are dragged into someone's pointless conflict?

I'd never seen him so angry! But he was right. We had been brought up to be independent and we lived a wonderfully settled rural life to that point. Suddenly, any control we had over our lives seemed to have been stripped away.

Chapter Three

September 1943 – Munich – South Germany

Less than three weeks later we found ourselves alongside the other young men from the village, arriving at the training camp in Munich. We were soon all allocated to different fighting units and began training in our groups. Johann and I were in different units and only bumped into each other at the end of the day in the dining area.

We didn't immediately get called forward to fight and our initial training period was extended for a while which was lucky for me, because it meant that I could take up the offer from the commander to return briefly to Maldorf to attend my planned wedding. He told me that he had received a letter from the village priest asking for me to be released for this event with Sophie. It meant just a few days back home and a chance to be with her again briefly and for us to share some intimate moments. I wasn't to know at the time, but this must have been when little Freddie was conceived.

It was good to share our Hochzeit with the family and a few friends in the village. Although everybody was still stunned by the events initiated by the war, just for a short while we were able to have a bit of fun, a few drinks and an opportunity to briefly forget our worries. The time went all too quickly before I had to drag myself away to join my colleagues in preparing for war.

It felt so strange to be kitted out in the full German

uniform, and then to feel so scared just a few weeks later when we were travelling in trucks to meet up with the other troops on the Belgian border.

When I eventually found myself on the battlefield, I was like a fish out of water. In the early days our officers did little to make the early war experience acceptable. We had been provided with second rate equipment and the food was so poor in comparison with what most of us had been used to. As we were marched from position to position, and made to endure the awful conditions of the dug-outs, these were the things that concentrated our minds.

One of the first things I learnt was to band together with the other Volksdeutsch. It didn't take long to realise that the soldiers who had been regular recruits and from mainland Germany were much more patriotic and supportive of the cause. When we had some free time, we would swap anecdotes about our various homelands. We were basically from all different parts of Europe. Until this time, I had been unaware that there were so many different ethnic German groups from so many separate states. Despite our far-flung heritage, a huge bond developed between us because we all felt regretful about being torn from our local communities.

This talk about our different homelands and our families and way of life, made the tedium and horrors of war more bearable. In my troop alone there were "Volksdeutsch" from Poland, Ukraine, Russia and Rumania. As I said, we were very different from those colleagues who had been recruited from within the Reich. Most of us had no sense of identification with the cause, whereas they had been subjected to years of Nazi propaganda and targeted information from the state media in the months leading up to the war.

We had to play this very low key because there was a certain fervour in the way the others would speak about the war. It was clear that in their communities the propaganda of Hitler had made a big impact in convincing them that this was a campaign worth fighting for. We had seen little of this in our remote towns and villages. This made it all the more shocking first to be called up and then to be thrust into fighting battles which we could not identify with.

Having been under attack for what seemed like months and having taken a load of casualties our troop was very demoralised. Wherever we moved our dugouts were bombarded mercilessly. I still have nightmares about some of the deaths I witnessed. Friends smashed to pieces; limbs separated from the bodies of fit young men. Stories they left behind about what they were planning to do when they returned home after the war.

The writing had been on the wall for some time that we were losing the war. We realised that at the highest level our leaders had conspired to set their sights too high and alienated too many powerful allies. On the front-line we had never been served well by our officers who increasingly became indecisive and failed to communicate with the troops in an effective way. Given that ours had not in any case been a campaign with a mission, morale sunk to a very low level. We Volksdeutsch lads had never bought into the idea right from the start and the more the campaign went on the more we felt disillusioned. Any thoughts of loyalty to Germany had long been knocked out of us.

Chapter Four

Late 1945

With hindsight, I now know that we were captured just before what the English came to call VE Day. When we were taken it was something of a relief to all of us in our troop.

It was several months after this that we eventually arrived as prisoners in England after a lengthy period spent in different holding camps. Johann and I were separated in the early stages of the war, and I had lost contact with him. At the final holding camp, I had been very closely interrogated before being posted to one of the hundreds of labour camps across England.

I had feared the worst when we set off in the trucks, heading north for somewhere in Cumbria. I had no idea at all where this was, but knew it was in the North of England. When I got there the first impressions of the camp was that it didn't seem as strict as I had anticipated. It was strange, of course, being incarcerated with twenty other guys in a cramped hut, but eventually we were allocated work placements and a sense of reality started. I was allocated to a local farm, and the work was tolerable and similar to what I had done in Maldorf.

One thing that I had been immediately struck by when I arrived in Cumbria, was the similarity of the surroundings to the landscape of my native Maldorf. I didn't know at the time that the stark fells to the east were the Pennines, nor that the beautiful hills to my west were the beginnings of the Lake District. What was different though, was that the fields there were filled with sheep not cows, and that the roads were so much better than the pot-holed cart tracks that ran through our village back home.

As the weeks went by, I noticed other similarities. The farmer, his wife and their children, were devout Christians and fastidiously went to church each Sunday. Back home our families invested a lot in the local Lutheran church and as children we all had to attend each Sunday. Once the farmer had learnt to trust us, he encouraged us to attend the church and most of the prisoners took up the opportunity to go, as it was another welcome break from life in the camp.

In the early days, before the work on the local farm became more regularised, life in the camp could be pretty boring. We were a motley group of individuals, coming from different parts of the so-called German empire. During our rest time, we would share stories about our upbringing and about our family back home, but generally there was very little to do. Things improved when we started to receive copies of "Die Wochenpost", which was a British Government-produced newspaper in the German language. It set out to provide a balanced view on the progress in the war but we were all suspicious about its true purpose. For this reason, I was a little sceptical about it at first, but at least it was giving me some information on what was happening outside the small world of the camp.

Later on, I remember receiving books translated into German from the YMCA. We got this peculiar list of available titles from the YMCA series entitled "Zaunkung Bucher". This seemed a little odd as this translated as "The Wren on a barbed wire fence!" Indeed, at the top was the image of the pretty little bird on the sharp fence. Nevertheless, despite the silly title, over time I remember reading from the works of Georg Bucher, Stefan Zweig and Herman Hesse! Who would have thought that whilst a prisoner my cultural knowledge would improve?

Looking back, I was probably the quietest of our group and as a result I think I gained the guards trust earlier than the rest. They could see that I was generally a calming influence if things were getting a bit tense in the group. After all, if you put twenty fellows together in one dormitory, at some stage there will be a falling out amongst them. It was generally about some petty issue that had started in the fields. Someone had not pulled their weight, or had said the wrong thing, and all hell would break loose. It never really got to fisticuffs as we had all been warned about bad behaviour and I guess we were all scared of being moved to somewhere a bit more punitive. At the end of the day, it didn't take me long to get the warring parties to realise how lucky our placement was.

Strangely, we didn't get much abuse from the locals when we first stepped out into the community to attend work. I suppose that this was because our camp was in quite a remate location and the country folk by nature were broadly tolerant people. We got the odd cursing from some of the local lads, but generally we were taken for what we were. So long as we were seen to behave, we were tolerated. The first time I went to the local church I was amazed not so much at the service, because there were the usual prayers, lessons and singing of hymns, but unlike Maldorf, the men and women were allowed to pray together. Back home the women and men were separated in church. The women prayed in the main body of the church whilst the men were above in stalls more akin to a theatre. Another difference was that here in Cumbria the men wore their best clothes to church and no two of them dressed alike. In Maldorf the men all went to church in their warm Afghan-type coats, whatever the weather.

Our work in the fields in Cumbria was arduous, but we were lucky to have a such a kindly farmer as our boss. He would allow us breaks and even bring us food and a bottle of beer when the weather was hot. This generosity upset his fierce wife. I recall that on one occasion when she brought him his sandwiches at lunchtime and saw that we were drinking beer. She laid into him and he stood just stood there and took it from her.

-   You're too bloody soft with the buggers. They don't deserve to be molly-coddled.

As she disappeared across the field, he turned to us, winked, put up two fingers and spat out:

-   Fucking cow.

214

At the time I didn't know how bad this language was, but understood he was abusing her behind her back. Years later I would get into trouble with Horst and Adi when I recalled the story to our English visitors and passed on the only phrase I had retained from my spell in England.

Each evening when we returned to the camp and after our meal, I would retire to the dormitory and think about earlier times. Invariably, I thought of Sophie and Freddie our child. I had received one letter from Sophie since arriving at the camp, delivered via the Red Cross, and in it she told me how they were getting on. Her parents were offering her support whilst she worked in the fields and earned money to keep them all going. She reminded me of the thoughts we had shared just before I left for the war. If I survived, we would try to set up a new life in Bavaria, where we had heard there was prosperity and good chances for our new family.

As the weeks went by in the camp, I felt starved of contact with my family. Very occasionally letters would arrive, and we would swap with each other what news came in. Nevertheless, this was a poor substitute for being able to speak to a loved one. As to the passage of the war, it was difficult to gauge where it was up to. We had heard murmurings of the bombing of Sheffield and Coventry, without knowing at the time that even greater damage was being inflicted on Nuremburg, Wurzburg and Dresden.

More disturbing was that towards the end of our

imprisonment we were made to watch some Pathe News film about the release of people from Auschwitz in January 1945. This left me with a strange mixture of embarrassment and shame. I could see what camp officials were trying to do; to get us to focus on the cost of the war and the insanity and cruelty of what the Nazi regime did. But of course, in my mind's eye, I had already come to realise this. These frightening images have stayed with me ever since.

In my free time, I would go back to think about home and the happy times that I had as a child living alongside Johann and his family. We were all very close, and shared the same lifestyles, interests and pastimes. We lived the simple yet fulfilling life that had passed down through the many centuries of history that our community had existed in Transylvania. I suppose that this Saxon heritage had instilled in its people a sense of family, of hard work, but also of tradition and culture. When we got home from work or school it was the family and our heritage which drew us together.

In Maldorf everyone was so hard-working during the day. The women used to meet up to cook together and knit their clothing and embroider the table linens and bed sheets. Come September, all the ex-Maldorf women would gather masses of cabbages together and help each other in the task of preparing sauerkraut for the coming winter months. As a young child tasting the first batch of sauerkraut each year and being allowed the thick skin off the buffalo milk were treats that I especially remember. After work the men would also get together and prepare the schnapps on their home-made stills and then take great delight through the year visiting each other to taste the fruits of their labour.

Later when we were able to return to Germany, we clung onto this heritage. Just as in Rumania, when we settled in Germany we would meet in each other's homes and chew the fat over a glass or two of Schnapps. The men would retire to the garden or the cellar, share their drinks and solve all of the day-to-day problems. The women would join together in cooking and baking and meeting up to share a coffee and cake. Later when we had settled more in Bavaria, the conversation between the men turned also to work and football and politics. In more modern times our children would think that this was all very sexist, but the older generation who had survived the war found it hard to change behaviours.

Once in Germany, we eventually had to change our ways of making schnapps. In Maldorf the men all made their own versions, using mainly grapes, in their own stills. These distilling techniques, and the home-made equipment, had been passed down through the generations. In Germany, we found that eventually it was illegal to brew spirits in this way and therefore we had found ways to carry on with the tradition without being found out. Each person kept a part of the equipment that made up the still. Each month we used to gather in turn in a chosen person's cellar, each bringing our own piece of kit, before assembling it and starting the process. In turn, over time everyone got to have a batch of schnapps, and the process would begin over again.

Chapter Five

Gersthofen – early 1948

  The journey to setting up my base in Bavaria was a long and complicated one. Although the war had officially ended in 1945, most prisoners were seen as being vital to the re-building process in England and were kept on to work. The main aim was to help the country build up the food stocks that were so depleted after the war. I began to lose heart as I grieved more and more about my separation from Sophie and our child. The farmer who I worked for from the camp was so kind to me, and hearing my plight, advised me that, given my special circumstances I could apply for compassionate discharge.

  He and his wife helped me write a letter outlining my case. I spelt out the need for me to return home to fight for the release of my wife and to re-patriate my son. It seemed ages before I got a reply as the system seemed so time-consuming and bureaucratic. I guess it took the best part of 1947 before someone from the War Office visited me in the camp and asked me loads of questions. They were very similar to those I had answered at the reception centre at Kempton Park when I arrived as a prisoner of war in England. Not surprisingly, with the help of positive comments from the farmer, I got the same "A" grading as before. Clearly, they still saw me as a low-risk prisoner.

  As it turned out, I only just beat the eventual mass re-patriation decision by a few months, but at least it meant that in early 1948 I was finally told I could leave the camp. Things then all happened very quickly. The farmer came to me one day and said that I was to be taken by truck to Hull for a ferry journey to a place called Cuxhaven which was a small port in North Germany. From there I would be transported to a holding camp before being allowed to head for my chosen place in Germany.

Next day I was told that they would be picking me up that afternoon, and that I would be allowed to pack a few personal items, including some food and cigarettes, but no English currency. I was told that a note would be made of how much of my savings I had handed over to the camp leader, and that I would eventually get what was owed to me in German currency, plus a small allowance when I arrived at the demobilisation camp in Munsterlager in North Germany.

The boat journey took about twenty-four hours and the truck journey to the camp about two hours. I wasn't there long, probably two days, during which time my discharge papers were signed and stamped and I was given forty Reichsmark to cover discharge pay and what I had been owed from the camp. I was taken with others by truck to the railway station and then effectively I was on my own.

Once at the station with my solitary suitcase, I started to check possible destinations that would get me as close to South Germany as possible. My first stopping point when I eventually got onto the train was at Hanover. Here I had to change trains for Frankfurt by which time it was getting dark, so I found a cheap guest house near to the station and stayed the night. The landlady was very kind to me and insisted that she provide a modest supper and then breakfast in the morning.

From there, the next train journey took me to Stuttgart and then finally I was able to get a train to Munich. Just as I had been leaving the camp back in England, Joseph Franks, the allocated translator, had provided me with a bit of information about work opportunities in South Germany. He wrote down some notes for me which he said might be useful when I arrived in Germany. He didn't need to have done this, but we had become friends, I think because he identified with my story about Sophie and Freddie. He had a wife and young son, and I guess he took my story to heart. It was so touching that even with his Jewish background he was still prepared to offer help to a German.

When we last spoke, as I was about to leave, he had pointed out to me that there was a lot of potential work in the city of Augsburg, which was about fifty kilometres away from Munich. He mentioned that it had escaped the major bomb damage that other cities had experienced and that there was in particular a large chemicals factory there which might be a good place to look for work. As I was sitting on the train, I noticed that there was a route map on the carriage wall opposite me. I could make out that the train stopped at Augsburg before it finished its journey into

221

Munich. I had got talking to this chap on the train who was heading for Munich and he said that the Hoechst chemical plant was in fact situated in a place called Gersthofen. I couldn't believe my luck, because on the map there was a stop shown there just after Augsburg, so there and then I decided to make that my destination.

When I hopped off the train onto the platform at Gersthofen, I took out the notes that the interpreter had given to me. It mentioned that the new German government had said up information centres in most cities and towns to help with re-patriation. I asked about this at the customer service desk when I got off the train and rather brusquely the receptionist pointed me in the right direction towards the Rathaus. She said that this was my best option. In the Town Hall I was met again by a rather prickly response and I was asked to show my papers confirming my status as an ex-prisoner of war. I was relieved to find out that this afforded me help towards re-settling. I was given an address to stay on a farm where I would get some temporary employment, plus a small amount of money from the State to get me started. This was much needed as my original small amount of cash had just about run out.

After the rather muted response that I had got on my initial arrival I didn't feel very optimistic for the future. I had expected some sympathy on my arrival in Germany and an understanding of what I had been through, but instead there was a good deal of resentment from the local population. They seemed to resent people like me coming into their community and taking away jobs and resources. I hadn't realised that the war had led to serious hardship amongst the working population as the new State struggled to pay the cost of being at war for so long.

However, things looked up a bit when I arrived at the farm in Bauernstrasse, on the edge of the small town. The farmer was reasonably friendly and he explained that I would be joining a group of refugee workers on the farm. In return for working on the farm I would get food and modest accommodation. There was a sort of bunkhouse shared with half a dozen other workers with a shower room and space to put belongings. Not that I had much at that stage. I was pleased to a degree because farm work was what I had been brought up to do and I decided that it would keep me going for a while. However, I was determined to try to find something better and earn enough to try to have a place of my own for when Sophie and Freddie could join me.

What actually happened was that I stayed for longer than I had initially planned because eventually the farmer offered me a more responsible job on the farm. He must have seen that with my background I could be trusted with more responsibility and with this my pay increased, plus I had minimal expense because as part of the job he provided me with a small cottage on site. Another advantage to being in Gersthofen was that I discovered that there were other ex-Maldorf families living in the area, with similar experiences to mine. This provided me with some social outlet and would prove invaluable later when I looked to find a place of my own.

During this period, I found the work and the life on the farm rewarding and the time I spent there provided a chance to get my thoughts together for the future. In the early days I was able to send off a letter to Maldorf to see if there was any news about Sophie, but when I finally got a reply it did not make good reading.

Dear Hans,

Thank you for letting us know of your latest address and it is good for us to hear from you and to know that you are alive and well. Also thank you for bringing us up to date about Johann and his decision to stay in England. We are so happy for the two of you as you seem to have a plan for the future. We were more worried as the war progressed and wondered whether we would ever hear from you again.

We still have not got over the shock of our young people being sent to the labour camps in Ukraine. I think all the time of how our beautiful daughter Katherina is getting on. She is so vulnerable. This has also been especially cruel for your Sophie who was separated from Freddie so soon after he was born. We pray each day with the priest Herr Unger, that our young people will be allowed home from the camps. The priest is a good man and his daughter has also been taken away. He has been doing all he can to find out information for us and the rest of the village.

We have not heard anything direct from any of them and in fact the only information we have had is from the very few who have returned here due to sickness and ill-health. They have told of the inhumane conditions and of work that is unbearable at times. Some, they told us, had not survived and died whilst in the camps.

It is not very pleasant here in Maldorf at the moment. The Russians seem to want to blame us for all the sins of the Nazis and are making life very difficult for us here. Our land and property have been seized and handed over to local Rumanian families. We are lucky that we have been allowed to stay in part of our house and for a rent we can carry on working our fields and tending the animals. Others have not been so lucky and have had to move away to try to set up a new life.

If we could we would come and join you in Germany, but our leaders are powerless now to help us. We continue to do our best for little Freddie and keep talking to him about you and Sophie. We all must hope and pray that these troubles will soon end.

Love,

Your Loving Mum

Chapter Six

July 1949

Although I had been deeply troubled at the news from Maldorf, it doubled my resolve to move forward and build something positive for the future when Sophie and Freddie could re-join me. My plan was to find a job which would pay more and allow me to save towards acquiring my own accommodation for when I could be re-united with my wife and child. Having got to know me over time the farmer and his wife were very sympathetic to my cause and said that they would eventually help me find a better paid job if I could find a replacement for the farm.

However, events took a turn for the better shortly afterwards and all thoughts of a new job were put aside when I received exciting news via the Red Cross. They still had my details from earlier and contacted me to let me know that Sophie and her sister Sara had turned up out of the blue in a town further north having somehow managed to escape from their camp.

I never really knew the details of what had happened to Sophie in the labour camps, or the suffering she felt at being separated from Freddie for so long. I'd had no means of knowing even where she had been sent, let alone write to her so I was shocked that day when I received a letter from the Red Cross saying that Sophie and her sister Sara were in Nuremburg, and would be arriving in Augsburg in two days' time. The letter briefly said that they had entered western Germany, following a period of internment in a camp on the Russian side of the border. I was requested to meet them at a given time at Augsburg station.

Of course, it was a very emotional moment when I met them on the platform. There was no attempt at explanations as we were just caught up in the moment. Later, I tried to get Sophie to talk about what had happened to her and her sister whilst they were away in the camps, but she would not speak about this in any detail. Sara was the same whenever I tried to broach the subject with her in the future. The two of them just did not want to talk about it, and in the end, I just backed off.

One thing that had shocked me when I saw Sophie on the platform for the first time after so long, was just how frail she looked. When I had last seen her, she had been the strong and robust young woman that I had grown up with in Maldorf. So, in the early days of meeting up again in Gersthofen, we initially focussed on getting back to know each other and then eventually to plan how we might get Freddie to join us in Germany.

Every day we thought of how best to achieve this. We wrote to the Rumanian Embassy explaining our position. Months went by before we even got a reply. They said they were looking into it and would get back in due course. For months nothing happened so we asked our relatives back in Maldorf to push harder at their attempts to get him re-patriated. I think what eventually paid off was our persistence and the endless barrage of correspondence from both within Germany and at the Maldorf end. Having said that, it was not until 1958 that Freddie arrived by train with other children whose parents had established themselves in this part of Germany. We had received news of this from our local Mayor and were so excited to travel to meet Freddie at the train station in Augsburg. By then our son was fifteen years old and having not seen either of us for so long, it was some time before we were all able to adjust. A letter from Sophie's parents in Maldorf, also confirmed the information that the mayor had received. Everybody's persistence had paid off.

Dear Hans,

I have just received the fantastic news that Freddie is being allowed to return to Germany to meet up with you and Sophie. I have been sharing your letters and photographs with him and he is so excited at the prospect of seeing you both. At this end we were fortunate in that one of my cousins had been voted in as a senior party member in the local headquarters at Tigor Mures, and he has been able to plead our case. We have been given the date of June 15th as the day he will be leaving on a train with other children who are also to be re-patriated.

Their train is fairly direct through to Munich, and then there is a change onto the Augsburg train. He has been told to get off at the Gersthofen stop, the penultimate station before Augsburg. Please write back to let us know that you have received this letter and will be there to meet him.

Your loving Mum

Strangely, when we eventually met Freddie on the station platform, having been separated for all those years, it was as if we had not been apart. We were all very emotional and flung our arms around each other. There were bucket loads of tears. Whilst all this had been going on our plans for the future had been largely put on hold. Sophie had come to live and work alongside me on the farm and we took Freddie back with us to pick up the pieces on our family life.

It took the best part of two more years before we could start to establish a place of our own. True to his word, the farmer helped me find a job driving trucks, which is what I had been trained to do during my spell in the army. Not that I actually spent much time in trucks as for the most part we were keeping our heads down and avoiding the enemy. I also found some additional work for a local builder in Gersthofen, so I was earning good wages. Sophie also earned a small wage assisting at the farm. I was able to get Fred employment with the builder and he was able to train as a bricklayer which gave him a sound trade for the future. As a result, between us we were able to put together quite a healthy pool of savings.

Through the local Siebenburgen group we developed friendships and we were able to re-unite with other Maldorf families. We had known the Zikeli family back home and had been good friends, so it was no surprise when Georg Zikeli and I decided to pool our resources and build a house for our families together. After an initial period of time renting a property in Mozart Street in Gersthofen, we found a plot on Peter Dorfler Strasse which had enough room for two maisonettes and a reasonable sized garden. We were to occupy the ground floor and they the upstairs. True enough, that is exactly what happened and we all contributed the funds for the project. Fred, Georg and I did the bulk of the building work with some help from other friends when it was required. Fred and Georg's son Horst had been re-patriated together from Maldorf and had become close friends. Horst was more studious and therefore didn't get involved so much in the building as he built a separate career in finance.

I have to thank Sophie for her patience through these strange times for making the process as smooth as possible. She continued to say very little about her bad experiences and just learnt to cope with the injuries that she had sustained whilst away. She concentrated all her efforts into bringing us all back together as a family and for that I am eternally grateful. We had a few moments along the way when we disagreed a little about Sara and her way of life. I couldn't accept the different relationships that Sara had with men who I had little regard for. I tried to support her as best I could but ultimately my relationship with Sara fell apart. I know it caused Sophie heartache but I only did what I felt was best for all parties. Freddie developed a strong relationship with Sara which never wavered even through her worst periods. He continued to visit her and I think this helped her cope with the trials that kept cropping up in her life. Perhaps he saw me as stubborn for not being more forgiving to her and it created a bit of tension between us which I greatly regretted. Eventually Freddie married and continued his work and family life in a nearby town.

Chapter Seven

January 2017 - Gablingen

More than ever now I look back and remember the happy times when we had visitors from England. As I take a look through this photograph album with its strange black and white prints and crumpled edges, I notice a very unusual photograph. The clothing that everyone was wearing throws me initially, but then I remember. It was one of the occasions when Johann's son Johnny brought his girlfriend Joy to visit, alongside his brother Paul. There we all were in the picture, dressed up in a strange set of black dungarees with a red fez on our heads. Suddenly the penny had dropped and I recalled that this had been taken as we were about to descend into the salt mines near Salzburg! How strange that was because we all had to sit on a long flume which then hurtled us underground where we could explore the salt-lake on boats.

Most of the time we were all happy to see each other and catch up on our lives but one incident sticks out though, which was a bit challenging at the time. I think it must have been on one of Johnny's visits when he was in his late teens. As usual we were trying to find out what places he would like to see during his stay, when suddenly he blurted out:

- Could we go to see Dachau? My German teacher has recommended a visit and I think it is nearby.

The other family members in the room were shocked at the request. Johnny was clearly innocently unaware of the enormity of what he was asking. After the initial stunned silence, Freddie spluttered out his annoyance, but thankfully in the Sachsisch dialect that we all spoke when we were together. This was a million miles away from the limited text book German that our guests had acquired. Although they didn'tunderstand the colourful language he was expressing, they couldn't but fail to recognise his anger and annoyance.

Over the years, as a family we had been torn about how to deal with the embarrassment that we felt about the war years. Of course, when it all started, we were just getting on with our lives in Rumania. Then we had been dragged into the war and had to endure our own dreadful experiences. Despite this now, as naturalised German citizens, we somehow felt some kind of responsibility for the atrocities committed by Hitler. Looking back, this had just been a naïve request that Johnny had made, clearly not thinking about the sensitivities involved.

When he dropped his request into the conversation it was indeed as if a bomb had exploded into our quiet world. After the initial shock waves, an eerie silence stopped everyone in the room in their tracks. Johnny and his girlfriend had just arrived from the railway station and we were all assembled to greet them in the living room. Beers and pleasantries were being shared by all family members.

- How was the journey
- How is everyone back home?"

Then that fateful request!!

After this initial difficult period, I quickly changed the subject and we all retreated back into our pleasantries and small talk. The tension was relieved to a degree but it stayed in the background for the next few days while we decided what to do about this request which had shocked us all. It was my decision finally to go ahead with the visit even though Freddie remained angry and Johnny acutely embarrassed. We still hung on to the view that although the war had ended all those years ago, we personally were somehow to blame and that our English relatives might have some residual resentment. As indeed we sensed might have the whole of the British nation.

However, through this incident we came to realise that our English relatives in fact bore no such malice. Their own clear innocence and embarrassment about the situation told its own tale. Nevertheless, I decided that it was best to try to overcome the defensiveness that we had shown. I asked myself why had we not visited Dachau in the past? It was only thirty minutes down the motorway in the car.

When we got there, the sights in the war museum really shocked all of us. We walked into rooms full of horrific photographs of emaciated prisoners, in the same awful uniforms. As we moved through the galleries the facts and figures were truly appalling; the numbers who went through the camp and the very few people who survived the experience struck home and as we walked the tension rose amongst the group. No words were spoken but we all I am sure felt the pain and the tragedy that occurred in the guise of warfare.

Outside as we moved closer, the buildings became more horrific and we saw the vast chambers where towards the end of the camp's life many bodies were cremated. By this time, I was feeling a mixture of shame and embarrassment that this could have happened in our country. I was also ashamed that we had put this to the side as the country had risen after the war and grown successful and industrious. Strangely though, when we got home and over the next few days of the visit this truly horrendous experience seemed to have a cathartic effect on all of us on both sides of the family. It was as if a big load had been lifted. We could see that Johnny had not intended to cause pain and embarrassment. He was not seeking to make a point. From his point of view, he could see clearly that we were appalled at the atrocities committed on both sides in the war. He knew that our side of the family had suffered privations and suffering both through the war and in the years afterwards. No more was said, but our family bonds were somehow stronger.

There was one other visit in 1988 that stood out also for me. That year, Johnny brought his own children to join us, and from our house in Gablingen we planned to visit Maldorf to show them where the family history had begun.

Being a hard-line communist state, the trip to Rumania proved to be an enlightening experience for them. No surprise to Sophie and myself of course because we had made a few trips back home to see family and to take them much-needed medicines and goods which were difficult to get there. The journey and transit into the country in those days was not to be under-estimated, particularly for such a large party. Johnny and Joy had come with their two children and brought along Johnny's brother Paul and his girlfriend Sara too. Sophie and I led the way in the family car, followed by Horsti and Adi, plus Johnny's entourage, in the Ford Passenger vehicle that I had hired for the occasion. Every spare place in the vehicles was crammed full of food, clothing, medicines and chocolate goodies, which were later to prove essential for smooth passage over the border into Rumania. There was still such a shortage of materials in Maldorf that I intended to get as much to them as I could.

What a journey it turned out to be as we set off from Gablingen around midnight. We travelled through Bavaria into Austria, taking a break after about six hours. From here we crossed fairly smoothly into Hungary, heading for the best crossing point into Rumania at Arad. It was at this point, when we hit the Rumanian border, that my plan to stock the vehicles with goodies suddenly made sense to the English guests. Painfully slowly we moved in the queue forward towards the border, only to be stopped once again by guards who wanted to see our papers etc. I knew also that the stops were designed to give the guards a chance to extort something from each visiting party. At each stop I would dip into my reserves of chocolate and cigarettes and give the guards a small bribe. I knew from previous experience, that this was the only way to make progress.

At one point, about six hours into this debacle, Paul decided to play his trump card, waving his British passport and saying very abruptly to the armed guard, "We are British citizens, you cannot treat us like this". Swiftly, I managed to pull him away and more bribery eventually got us through. Once over the border, we had to travel another three hours or so in the early hours and our guests were struck by the darkness experienced as we first went through the city centre and then by the number of horse-drawn carts we saw being guided by a light at the front of the carriage. Horst explained later to our guests about the city darkness; about the power cuts that the government imposed to preserve scarce fuel and electricity. He had jokingly warned the visitors that Rumania would seem to them like a Third World country and they were beginning to understand what he meant.

As we neared our destination dawn was breaking and we saw men and women walking along the side of the road with their crude farm implements, obviously walking miles to their places of work. I think our visitors were all shocked by the standards that existed at that time and during the visit it was difficult to get Johnny's young children to understand why there was nowhere to find an ice-cream or a can of coca cola.

It proved to be quite a momentous visit for Johnny in particular. We had arrived at the house in Maldorf late at night and had been shown to our rooms by Sophie's sister Maria as this was now her family house. It was pitch black because there was no electricity in the property. In the morning Johnny came towards me excitedly and took me into the bedroom in which he had slept. He pointed to the wall, and there hanging was a framed photograph of a young Johann in his farming gear with long leather boots. I think that this one experience alone brought home to him the importance of the visit. The young children struggled a bit with the privations that they had to bear and with the scorching heat. Nevertheless, for the adults the visit proved to be a big success and everywhere we went in the village we were met by kindness and generosity. The families we met had very little to give but what they had they shared with us.

I also remember the happy visits that Horsti and Adelheid arranged for subsequent visits from England. They came back excitedly from one memorable trip to the mountains with Johnny and Joy when the children were still young. They had driven down to the Austrian border and had rented a log cabin near to a place called Ruhpolding. Horsti was so keen to tell me about the trip and one moment seemed to stick out for him. They had taken the cable car to the top of the Zugspitze which at nearly 10000 feet is Germany's highest mountain. On the way up a fierce thunderstorm had struck and the cabin had got stuck on one of the pylon-supports that stretched all the way up the mountain. After some initial angst they watched the operator dangle out of the cabin and poke the metal cable with a long pole until finally it was freed. Fear turned to joy as the cable-car sped upwards on the final part of the journey.

Once at the top Horst explained that they had eaten some schnitzel and chips, washed down with a beer and then had decided to walk all the way down the mountain. By the time they had got three-quarters of the way down three-year-old Anna's little legs must have been tired because she insisted on her dad hoisting her up onto his shoulders. From her lofty perch, with a chuckle, she said;

-   Whose idea was this anyway?

For the rest of the holiday Horsti couldn't stop gleefully repeating this phrase and it brought a giggle every time from Anna and Jonathan.

Yes, I have so many other happy memories of their visits. Sophie and I took them to some beautiful places such as the castles of Linderhof, Nueschwanstein and Hohenschwangau. They were all such magical magical places. We even took a trip to the infamous Kehlsteinhaus or Eagles Nest at Berchtesgaden, where Hitler had built his mountain hideaway, perched on top of the mountain at just over 6000 feet up in the Bavarian Alps. Although this had been the Fuhrer's favourite place, and was undoubtedly very picturesque, everyone had mixed feelings about the place. It felt a little unreal, with its café set right on the top of the mountain. I didn't say anything but at the time it made me wonder what awful plans must been drawn up within the confines of the building. I am very grateful for all these happy memories which warm my heart as I get old.

Chapter Eight

Gablingen – February 2017

I am too frail now to stroll out of the house and venture into the forest. Nowadays, I receive my satisfaction from seeing Horsti and Adi striding out with their strange Nordic walking poles, or riding their mountain bikes to explore the many tracks which lace the forest. Most days they go walking as I used to, across the fields, into the woods and beyond. Occasionally they go further afield. When they take their walking poles it makes me laugh at this strange walking style, so different to how Sophie and I used to amble slowly along those same paths. When our visitors came to stay from England, we shared these same walks and revelled in the joy they had in enjoying the local fields and forest.

In those days, we would pause briefly to sit in front of the little white chapel on the hill by the side of the woods. Further on, we would look through the railings into the summer gardens and large private plots that had been fenced off in the woods. These were the weekend retreats of wealthy Augsburg families. In one of them, as we walked past, sometimes a Rotweiller dog would come ferociously up to the fence, barking to warn us off. We were very grateful for the secure fence that separated us! Further on there was even a plot where the amateur theatre group from the city came, with a little outdoor amphitheatre, where they would practice their latest masterpieces.

Our visitors never seemed to tire of these walks and would often take off themselves to explore different paths. I remember on one occasion they came back really excited as they had come across a secret paddock that existed deeper in the forest and where on this occasion the local riding clubs had come together for a gymkhana. It's strange, that although I am now nearly 100 years old, I can still look back and remember events of the past as if they were just yesterday. If only I could remember more recent things in the same way, then perhaps Horst and Adelheid would not have their patience tested by my forgetfulness.

Epilogue

Gablingen – March 2017

Johnny and his wife gather with others outside the old church in Gablingen. The weather is cold for the time of year and there is a piercing blue sky which is almost like a blessing. They had planned to visit in June but sadly have had to make their journey prematurely as Hans has died just three months short of his 100th birthday. Now like the other guests they stand here in quiet sadness, alongside Han's son Horst and his wife, Adelheid.

Suddenly, the great oak doors to the old church open and the crowd snakes deferentially in. The minister takes care to describe the main points of Hans long life. Prayers are taken and hymns sung and then the crowd move out of in line. They gather in the precincts of the church and then follow in pairs behind an old lady who carries a large ceremonial cross at the front of the procession. Somehow, for one so seemingly frail, she manages to bear the great weight, as the line of people moves through the village towards the nearby cemetery.

Cars stop in respect as they cross the street, and as the procession enters the cemetery, a brass band strikes up the music that for hundreds of years has played for others at their burial in the villages of Siebenburgen. Horst whispers to Johnny that the group of aging players are all originally from Maldorf. As the coffin is lowered into the grave, the guests queue up to throw roses on to the coffin followed by a small shovel-full of earth. A new marble headstone is in place showing that Hans is laid alongside his beloved Sophie. Later the crowd moves on, heavy-hearted, to the local Gasthof to eat and drink in respect to their loved on.

Across the room different generations chat and share memories of Hans. There are those in their eighties who had been brought up in Maldorf and survived the war years. They recall how life after the war in Rumania had been tough and how the communist years had seen their beloved village deteriorate, their years of work destroyed and their traditions eroded. Through the darker years they had stuck it out and taken their chance when it came to move to Germany.

Their children and grandchildren now live very different lives but have never forgotten their family roots. Even now with their parents they are planning the coming year's annual gathering of people from Maldorf and other Siebenburgen villages. This year they will meet in Dinkelsbuhl to celebrate the past, to re-kindle old memories and to keep the traditions alive. That spirit of being, that determination to survive, lives on in the room through the memories of Hans, Johann, Sophie and Sara. You can feel the buzz as their names echo proudly in the conversations at each table around the room. Spontaneously the singing starts:

-   Siebenbergen, Blessed Land
    Land of Plenty and of Strength
    Protected by Carpathian Mountains

    . . . .

The hall echoes to the joyful sounds as verse after verse rings out as the generations join together in remembrance.

Acknowledgements

Many thanks go to my German family for helping me realise my dream of recording the experiences of our family during and after the Second World War.

My cousin Elisa has shared my passion and whose energy throughout has continued to inspire me to finish. Towards the end we joked about sprinkling small pieces of gold dust to brighten the story; detail and events that I could not have uncovered without her help. Thanks also to her sister Hildegard and other friends for adding vital details.

Thanks also to my cousin Horst for assisting with information relating to his parents and to his lovely wife Adelheid who shared vital information about early life in Maldorf and Hohndorf, and details of Siebenburgen traditions.

Special note needs to be made of the contribution made by my life-long friend and fellow writer Don Rhodes. His feedback on the drafts, his highlighting of key reference documents, plus his translation skills have been invaluable.

Thanks also to my other Beta readers; my cousin Margaret Pratt; my friend John Handley; Charlie Heathcote; my wife Joy Winkler. Joy has patiently provided the encouragement and literary insight for me to produce something that resembles a work that I can be proud of.

Thanks to Anna and Jez de Silva for their design work.

Glossary

UK Prisoners of War: At the peak there were around 400,000 German prisoners in camps in England immediately after the Normandy Landings in 1944.

Volksdeutsche: In Nazi German terminology these were "People whose language and culture had German origins but who did not hold German citizenship". For centuries before many such communities had been dispersed across Europe, for example in the Baltic states, former Yugoslavia, Volgan states, Czechoslovakia, Poland, Hungary and Rumania.

Siebenburgen; In modern day Rumanian territory German "Saxons" were first encouraged to settle by the Hungarian kingdom between the 11th century and the end of the 13th century. They congregated around the town of Hermanstadt, which is modern day Sibiu. This is in Transylvania and their land became known to them as "Siebenburgen" meaning "Seven Fortresses". They developed their own dialect known as "Sachsisch" which survives today.

In the 1930 census there were just over 237,000 Germans in Transylvania which was 8.5% of the population.

Printed in Great Britain
by Amazon

77304555R10147